THE SECRET LIFE OF

AN ASSASSIN

DEIADRA NICOLE

E-book: ISBN: 979-8-9877100-0-5

Paperback: ISBN: 979-8-9877100-1-2

Hardback: ISBN: 979-8-9877100-2-9

Acknowledgments

This book would not be possible if it were not for my lord and savior and the many blessings and favor that he bestowed upon me. I want to thank my children (David and Darriel) for their continued love and support. I knew there were times when they did not understand me or the process, but through it all, they remained supportive, always encouraging me to follow my dream. I would also like to thank my editor and publisher-Beloved, cover design-Shoaib, and copyrights, for helping me to make this book a success. Last but certainly not least, I would be remiss if I did not thank everyone that showed their support.

Contents

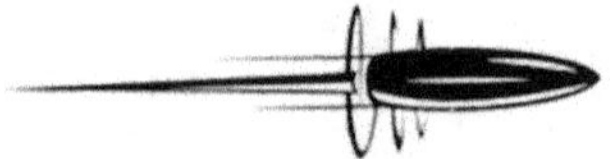

Introduction

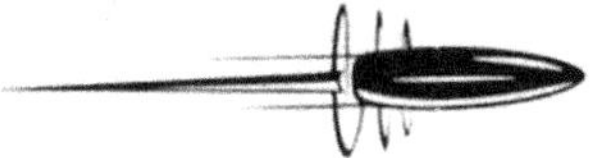

This book is a fictional novel about a family of assassins. A young girl named Jewel from the south decides to attend college upstate. She is faced with financial hardship as she struggles to find her way. She finds herself in an unforeseen tragedy that will forever change her life. The tragedy teaches her things about herself that she never otherwise would have known. Jewel meets Rellik El'Poep, the love of her life. Rellik and Jewel El'Poep are brought together by the tragic event where ultimately, they raise a family of assassins. The family struggles to keep their identity as assassins concealed but are constantly faced with adversities. They try to live their lives like an ordinary American family. The problem lies they aren't sure what is considered ordinary, they have only known life as assassins. They are constantly reminded that they are anything except ordinary. The family is a magnet for trouble, but as a family, they always seem to rise above their struggles.

Chapter 1:

The Early Years

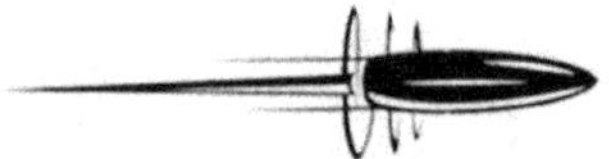

Jewel's Childhood

Jewel "Hunter" Huntington was born in a small country town in Georgia. She was the middle child among her seven siblings. Jewel's mother worked several odd jobs while her father worked as a contractor for a local trucking company. The Huntingtons had their fair share of trouble raising a family of seven, one boy and six girls. Her mother was constantly worried about being able to provide shelter and enough food for her family while her father battled with the demons of alcoholism. The Huntingtons lived in a low-income housing project. Jewel's parents were not wealthy, but they taught their children to be grateful regardless of their circumstances. Her parents believed firmly in disciplining their children.

The Huntington's did not allow their children to participate in several of the neighborhood's functions, just like many other neighborhood children. The Huntingtons did not want their children to be influenced by the negativity that oftentimes characterized many of the children that were raised in the projects. The Huntington's went to great lengths to ensure that the neighborhood in which they raised their children did not have a bearing on their lives and careers. The Huntington's kept a very watchful eye on their children. They demanded to know where their children were at all times as well as who they hung around. Growing up, Jewel was a very mild-mannered child. She, in many instants, got in trouble for her bullheaded ways. She was very stubborn and often stood out from her peers in the way she dressed and carried herself. She was stereotyped and misunderstood. She tried to fit in with the other children but always managed to stand out from the crowd. She eventually came to accept the harsh reality that she was vastly different from her peers. She not only embraced but began to take pride in knowing that she was significantly different from her peers and her siblings.

Jewel considered herself to be a trendsetter. She was strong-minded and strong-willed, and she would go to any length to achieve her goals in life. One would never know Jewel possessed such characteristics just by viewing her outward appearance or hearing her speak. She was painfully shy and very reserved. She was one who never got in a rush to do anything. Jewel took on her grandmother's mannerisms, who also happened to be a very soft-spoken and easy-going individual. Often, Jewel was sadly mistaken for being a pushover, at least **until you crossed her**. Jewel showed respect to everyone and, in return, demanded the very same respect. Jewel held those few that she called friends to remarkably high standards and had little patience for disloyalty of any sort. Jewel received several awards in grade school for her consistent politeness and overall superb mannerisms. Jewel's mannerisms are those of a true Southern Bell, as Southerners place high inferences on mannerisms. In high school, Jewel was voted most likely to succeed in her class. She participated in many activities in high school; she ran track and sang in the school's concert choir. She was recognized by Who's Who Among high school students.

She could never turn down a good game of basketball. She was one of the star basketball players for her school. Jewel had always wanted to go off to college in the hope of being recruited to play basketball professionally. Aside from playing professional basketball, she hoped to become a mechanical engineer someday. Jewel was good with her hands; she enjoyed designing and constructing things. Jewel's parents could not afford to send her to college. She was offered a four-year scholarship to play basketball for The University of Southern California (USC) after graduating from high school.

Her parents were immensely proud of her. The Huntingtons were incredibly grateful for Jewel having the opportunity to attend college despite their financial woes. She was excited about going off to college because it not only prepared her for adulthood, but she had never been out of the state of Georgia or on her own, for that matter. She had always been under the very watchful eye of her parents.

The Transformation

The Huntingtons and Jewel had spent twelve years planning for this moment. Jewel received the Valor Victoria award from her high school graduating class. She now hoped that college would be as easy as high school. She prepared all summer for college, and finally, the day came for Jewel to leave for The University of Southern California (USC). The moment she got off the plane in California, reality hit her like a sack of potatoes in the face. Jewel was overwhelmed with excitement as she walked down the sidewalk; she was in awe seeing the skyscrapers and other larger buildings than she was used to seeing. Jewel passed one girl who was her age, and she immediately spoke to her. The young girl looked as if she was looking through Jewel and continued on her way. Jewel, knowing how soft she spoke, assumed that the young girl did not hear her. Jewel thought to herself that when given the opportunity the next time, she would speak louder. After several failed attempts, she was quickly educated that speaking to an individual that she was not previously friends with was prohibited.

Jewel was now in a new state, an unfamiliar environment, and not being told who she could have as friends or where she was allowed to go was a very new experience for her. Jewel tries to adjust to her new life in a city larger than she could have ever imagined and adjust to a lifestyle much different than the one she had left behind. She would soon become a member of the school's sorority, where she would begin stepping in various step shows and attending parties on a regular basis. Her partying soon began to interfere with her classes. Jewel would soon begin arriving at her classes late. A tardy would soon turn into an absentee, and she was forced to withdraw from her classes or receive a failing grade due to her excessive absence. Jewel's grades began to fall drastically. She stopped going to her classes altogether, and she lost her scholarship. Jewel knew how proud her parents were of her for going off to college, and she could not disappoint them, her younger siblings who looked up to her, or even herself for that matter. So, Jewel knew that she had to decide whether to drop out of school or find the money to pay for college herself. Jewel knew she could not ask her parents for the money because things had just begun to look up for them, with four of their seven children being out of the house.

Chapter 2:

An Assassin Is Born

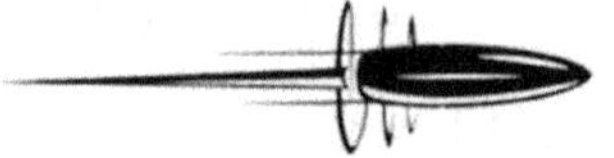

Financial Hardship

Jewel now considered herself a responsible adult capable of making adult decisions, and it was her responsibility to take care of herself. Her parents had grown older, and she felt that it was now her and her siblings' responsibility to provide and take care of their parents and their younger siblings. She decided that getting a job would be her best option. She applied for and got a job working for one of the local fast-food restaurants. Jewel was so far in debt that her salary would not be enough to pay her college tuition and her daily expenses. She was forced to work a second job. She began working for one of the local factories, but it would not be long before she was laid off.

Jewel, now had been laid off from one job and was not making enough money at her other job, refused to call her parents to ask for yet another handout. She reached out to her roommate Amy who enjoyed her job and always managed to have money. Jewel's roommate Amy worked as a dancer at the local Adult Entertainment Club. Jewel turned to Amy in a desperate attempt to get money. Jewel, a naive country girl from a small country town, interpreted many things differently than others. She thought that since she was in her high school's concert choir, where she danced 80 percent of the time, it would be a piece of cake for her. Jewel was unaware that the type of dancing Amy did was nothing like she had ever done before. Jewel's roommate Amy set up a meeting for Jewel and her boss, Mr. Gunz. Jewel was 5'7 and weighed 110 pounds. She was an athlete and, as a result, had always taken care of herself. Mr. Gunz, upon seeing Jewel, liked her and offered her the job instantly. Jewel would work for Mr. Gunz for several months. Mr. Gunz would soon start making increasing demands on his dancers to satisfy the growing needs of his customers.

The Tragedy

One day, one of the regulars requested to have one of the dancers perform at his private party for a large lump sum of cash. Mr. Gunz knew how badly Jewel needed the money. Mr. Gunz chose Jewel to perform for the private event. Jewel was told she would be picked up an hour after her shift ended in front of the club. An hour later, a black stretch hummer limousine would arrive to pick up Jewel. Upon entering the vehicle, she was blind folded immediately from behind. She was instructed not to remove her blindfold until told to do so. After driving for roughly an hour, the limousine finally came to a stop where Jewel was assisted out of the limousine and into the event. She was told that she was not to remove her blindfold under any circumstances, and she must not wonder out of the area assigned to her. After being instructed to remove her blindfold, Jewel stands in a room covered with white roses. Jewel was told that she could use the room in which she stood to get dressed for her performance.

When she has finished dressing, she is to knock on the door, and she will be escorted out onto the stage.

After getting dressed, Jewel knocks on the door, and she is blindfolded again and escorted through a poorly lit auditorium filled with men as they yell commands at her. Jewel is then escorted on stage in the spotlight and instructed to remove her blindfold. When she removed her blindfold, the music began to play, and she began to perform her adult dance arrangement. After her performance, Jewel was blindfolded again and escorted back to her dressing room, as they were extremely careful, making certain that she was unable to identify any of the guests. When she entered her assigned dressing room to change her attire, she noticed a gentleman, wearing a black pinstripe tuxedo with a black silk mask covering his face partially, watching her. Jewel uttered in her very softly spoken voice, "may I help you"? The man answered, "I sure hope that you can, for your sake," as he began to chuckle. The man insisted that Jewel get undressed and join him on the bed. When Jewel refused, he threw her onto the bed and began ripping her clothes off. What appeared to be a gun fell from the man's side onto the bed.

Jewel and the man began tussling for the gun when the gun accidentally discharged, striking the man in the chest. Jewel struggled to get dressed; she knew that she must leave. As she looked over her shoulder, she immediately spotted another man watching her. He is wearing a tuxedo like the victim's tuxedo but with a black silk mask covering his face partially but on the opposite side as the victim's face. The stranger told Jewel not to worry and that he saw everything and would help her get home safely. The man sneaks her out the back door, as he assists her with getting into his car, and gives her a ride home. The man introduces himself to Jewel as Rellik El'Poep. Rellik tells Jewel that he attended the party for business but laughs jokingly when he tells Jewel that he could not close the contract and his business trip was cut short due to Jewel's unfortunate incident. The incident would forever change Jewel's life. Jewel sat quietly in the car as she tried to make sense of everything that unfolded in front of her very own eyes. How could she have allowed this to happen? Is this the end of her life and career before it has even started? Jewel thinks that if she had only kept up her grades and not lost her scholarship, she may not have been involved in such an incident.

She also tries to make sense of Rellik's motive for helping her. Was Rellik pretending to help her and really planning to get revenge for his friend's death, or was the deceased man his enemy? Rellik warns Jewel that she must never speak a word about the incident to anyone ever. Rellik also explains to her that the individual she had killed was one of the most powerful drug lords that had ever exist. Rellik tells Jewel that he was contracted to murder the drug lord and was following him when the incident took place. Rellik tells Jewel that she must do as he says, making sure to follow all directions detail by detail, and she will be fine. Rellik informs Jewel that others would be coming in retaliation for the drug lord she had killed to avenge his death. He tells her that she is now a moving target. He warns her that even the confined walls of a jail cell would not save her life. Rellik vows to help Jewel but tells her that she must also get the proper training to be able to protect herself.

Rellik began working with Jewel daily to teach her self-defense techniques in case she was ever linked to the killing of the drug lord. While Rellik works with Jewel, he sees something special in her.

Jewel remained unbothered by the unfortunate event. It was like she had a niche for the life of an assassin. Jewel was quickly dubbed "Head-hunter," as her name speaks for itself. Hunter became one of the best in the game when it came down to Hunting for Prey, as she called it.

Until Death

Rellik compiled and gave Hunter a list of names. They had to assassinate everyone whose name was on the list in order to keep Hunter and her loved ones safe if the incident was ever linked to her. As time passed, the list got shorter until all hits were complete. Rellik and Hunter soon began taking paid contracts, and the risks became greater with each hit. Hunter would soon come up with her own strategy to perform hits. Hunter would eventually begin setting up and performing her very own hits. One day, when performing a hit, Hunter got comfortable upon performing the hit that she decided to sit down by the victim's body and have a glass of wine when the victim's girlfriend walked in and caught her. She was forced to perform an unauthorized hit on the victim's girlfriend to keep her cover from being blown.

Working together, Rellik and Hunter began to build a relationship that would soon blossom into a love affair.

A love affair that was pure and true, one that was both mentally and physically satisfying. Rellik and Hunter knew and understood one another because they knew one another's deepest and darkest secrets. Upon graduating from college, Rellik and Hunter decided to get married and start their very own family. Hunter would soon give birth to two boys that they named Ridge and Edge. Ridge was the youngest of the two children who were two years apart. Rellik and Hunter concluded that being contracted assassins had served its purpose because the job was very risky. Hunter and Rellik vowed never to tell a soul about their careers as assassins in fear of their families and children ever finding out. Hunter and Rellik now had enough money to live a life of comfort. Hunter finally got her mechanical engineering degree and now felt it was time to work in her career field. So, she began her job as a mechanical engineer. However, it took Hunter and Rellik some time to get used to their new lives.

Rellik would soon come to open his very own restaurant, and the El'Poeps would eventually move to the suburbs of California. Hunter wanted to give their children the type of lifestyle that she did not have as a child, but due to the recession of 2007, Rellik would soon have to close his restaurant. Hunter's hours would soon decrease to less than 20 hours per week. As a result, Rellik was left with no choice but to take what he could to try to support his family. Rellik often went out of town in search of work. Not long after these misfortunes, the company that Hunter was employed with also went out of business. The El'Poeps' need for money would soon become more of a demand as time passed. They soon began to fall behind on their bills. One of their cars would be repossessed as they would soon get a foreclosure notice on their home. It was obvious that their need for money was urgent. Late one night, Collin, the leader of the Justice League, gave Hunter a call, offering her a deal of a lifetime, one that she could not refuse. Hunter knew this was not the type of job that she wanted to grow old doing. Hunter knew she had been lucky up to this point because many of the League's members had been killed or even jailed.

She herself had come remarkably close to being killed in many instances. Collin explained to her that the success of this mission was crucial and that once completed, she and her children would never have to worry about ever wanting anything ever in life. Collin told Hunter that her houses, cars, boat, and children's college tuition would all be paid in full. This mission was held with high confidentiality. Collin explains to Hunter that they did not want to risk the possibility of the victim's information getting out, but she would get everything she needed at the time of the hit. The only information that was provided to Hunter was that the victim was a former member of the League that is now an informant for the enemy and must be stopped. The victim had lied to the league about performing a contracted hit that he, in fact, never carried out. Collin tells Hunter that she is chosen because he knows how she has an intolerance for disloyalty, and since she has been with the League, she has lived up to her name repeatedly as the "Head-Hunter." She accepted the assignment after much deliberation and decided to go for the hit. Everything went as planned.

Hunter was given the address where she was to meet Collin to get her assignment. Hunter pulls up in front of this beautiful mansion in the Hills of California, where Hunter is told to meet Collin to get more details about the assassination. In the details provided, she is to enter the mansion and go to the second floor. Hunter immediately gets chills. Hunter, at this point, had successfully completed many hits but never had such an uneasy feeling as she now had. Hunter is sweating and has butterflies in her stomach. She contemplated if she should leave or stay because it was a special assignment assigned. The assignment was given specifically to her by the leader of the League himself and, at this point, held in complete confidentiality. It was like deja vu, like she had been there before. In the instructions provided, Hunter was instructed to go upstairs, where she entered this beautifully decorated room filled with white roses. It all came back to Hunter that this was the same house and room where she had committed her first murder 15 years earlier. It looked and smelled just as it had 15 years ago, the night of the unfortunate incident that forever changed her life.

Hunter turned and was greeted by Collin. He begins to tell Hunter about the incident that took place there 15 years ago, and he tells Hunter that Rellik was paid for a job that he did not complete and that it was, in fact, Hunter that unknowingly completed the job. Collin tells Hunter how the League frowns upon liars and disloyal members and tells Hunter that Rellik was paid a large lump sum of cash for a job that he did not carry out. Hunter begins to explain to Collin when he cuts her off, explaining that they forgave Rellik for the incident because he recruited Hunter into the League as a result. He tells Hunter that she must kill Rellik because he has teamed up with the enemy and has shared many of the League's secrets, and planned to kill several of the League's members, and she may possibly be on his hit list. He explains that Rellik El'Poep is a contract killer and cares for no one. He tells her that Rellik El'Poep is not his real name and that Rellik El'Poep means Killer of People spelled backward. She must now kill him before he kills her and their children, or she will spend the rest of her life fearing for her and her children's lives. Collin tells Hunter that he has arranged a meeting for Rellik to meet him there, and she must kill him on sight.

Hunter is unsure of what to do, not knowing if Collin is telling her the truth. Hunter looks to Collin for answers. She asks him if this is true, why would Rellik want to destroy his own family? What reason could he have for wanting to kill them, and certainly, what benefits does he stand to gain? Collin stood staring out of a nearby window before turning to answer Hunter's question. "Head-Hunter, this is a new generation, and that means that the rules of the game have now changed. It is no longer just about money and power; one must also prove one's loyalty. Today, in many instances, you may be asked to kill someone you love and hold dearly to prove your loyalty. "Head-Hunter," I would strongly suggest you take my help to save yourself and your family while you can. We both know that Rellik, just like most assassins, is heartless and lets nothing or no one get in his way to get what he wants. Rellik would not hesitate to execute you and the family you have with him if it keeps him from getting what he wants." Collin told Jewel that she must act immediately because she had no time to waste. Collin decides to give Jewel more time to investigate Rellik so that she can confirm his claims.

Upon rescheduling their meeting, he says to her, "I can assume that you will contact me when you find out I am telling you the truth. I hope that it will not be too late."

The "Head-Hunter" was visibly shaken as she was escorted out of the back door. She was allowed to leave without performing the hit to conduct her very own investigation. The El'Poeps had always viewed death in a different light, being that they were contract killers most of their adult lives. Hunter had always played the role of the hunter and played it well, I might add, but now she is being hunted by one of their very own. She was asked to kill the man she loves and trusts with her deepest and darkest secrets or be killed. She could not understand what could drive her husband to want to kill her and the family that they had worked ridiculously hard to build, their two boys that were both splitting images of both of their parents, not to mention the countless sacrifices they made to give their children a better life than either one of their parents. For the first time in her life, she began looking at life and death differently. She decided that she would produce a plan of her own to get rid of Rellik if her investigation proved Collin's claims were true.

As Head-Hunter exited the back door of the mansion, she spotted Rellik going into the front door. If Collin was correct, this might be her first and possibly her last opportunity to kill Rellik. Head-Hunter immediately began investigating Rellik. She began looking at all his cell phone records and their bank accounts, as well as his new connections. "Head-Hunter" searched every place she could think of but never found anything that gave her the impression that Rellik was plotting to kill their children or herself. She concluded that Collin was making up the accusations to get her to turn against her husband to get back at him for leaving the league. Hunter confronted Collin, but he maintained that he was telling the truth and Rellik was waiting for the perfect time to assassinate his family as requested by his new powers-to-be. Hunter, unable to find any evidence on Rellik, keeps her guard up and continues to investigate him. Three months later, Hunter and Rellik are spending time together. As they lay watching television, Hunter has let her guard down because Rellik, at this point, has given her no reason to doubt him, and she has found nothing to prove Collin's claims.

Hunter begins to tell Rellik about Collin's claims. Rellik reassures Hunter that the claims are all false allegations and states that Collin is upset because he is no longer with the Justice League. Rellik tells his wife that the League wants to destroy him and their family. After Hunter leaves the room, Rellik stares out the window before getting a phone call. He informs the person on the other end of the line that there must be a change of plans because his wife has found out.

Chapter 3:

My Brother's Keeper

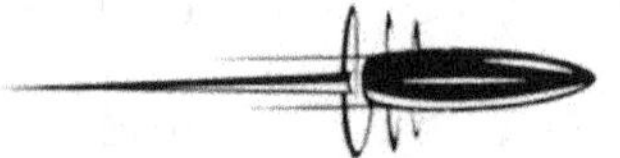

Visit From the Past

Ten years later, Rellik and Jewel's sons, Ridge, and Edge, are now young adults who, in many ways, take on their parent's characteristics. Ridge is very thin, just as his mother was in her childhood years, and has a style that is significantly different from others of his age. Ridge, just like his mother, was not the average young adult. His style was consistent with those individuals that are gothic/rap artists. Ridge, just like his mother, was very soft-spoken and very laid back. Edge, on the other hand, just as his name implies, is the very opposite; he is always on the edge. Edge seems like he is always in a rush as he is very adventurous, just like his father.

Edge likes to live life on the edge. Ridge and Edge both had an undeniable love for guns and hunting in general. Ridge will give you the shirt off his back, but Edge, on the other hand, will **take the shirt off YOUR back**.

The two boys are very opposite in character, but both are splitting images of each one of their parents. Ridge is quiet and reserved, and Edge, on the other hand, is loud and obnoxious. Ridge tried playing sports but found himself disinterested. He tried joining the school's marching band, yet again found himself not interested. In his spare time, he tried playing video games, but the only ones that captured his attention were the ones that contained violence. Eventually, he became disinterested in the gaming system.

The El'Poeps had a love for guns that was undeniable, and that was ultimately passed on to their children at a very early age. Ridge and Edge were well-educated about guns and rifles of all sorts.

Their children knew how to operate firearms of all calibers, blindfolded if necessary. Growing up, their parents always kept firearms in the family home. Finding a gun inside the El'Poeps' home was not out of the ordinary.

The El'Poeps tried to live a normal life but often found themselves struggling to overcome some old habits. The El'Poeps owned and operated a Wilderness Store that sold many supplies used for hunting and hiking. Next door to the Wilderness Store, they also owned and operated the neighborhood's first and only Wildlife Restaurant/Eatery. They cooked and sold cuts of meat from animals such as deer, squirrels, raccoon, opossum, frog legs, snakes, and wild hogs, to name a few. Rellik taught Ridge and Edge survival skills such as hunting and hiking at an early age. Rellik felt that teaching his sons how to hunt was a life skill that would be forever beneficial. Rellik never went any place without his gun. Likewise, Ridge and Edge also got into the habit of never going any place without their guns. Ridge was more discreet, but Edge, on the other hand, carried his black 500 Smith and Wesson Magnum gun with silver trimming on his side that he nicknamed "Do Something." Edge having a gun gave him a rush; it was a feeling of empowerment.

Edge enjoyed hunting, and he was a thrill seeker. Hunting for Rellik not only put food on the table but also gave him a sense of relaxation.

One afternoon, while working in the Wilderness Store, Ridge ran into another young man whose name was Ruben, which shared the same interest as him. While shopping for supplies, Ruben began talking to Ridge about his love for hunting and invited him to go hunting with him. Ridge was initially skeptical because he had only hunted with his brother or his father and no one else. Ridge's love for hunting would not allow him to refuse the offer. Ruben and Ridge made plans to meet on the first day of the hunting season. They planned to hunt wild hogs and deer.

Ruben and Ridge are talking as they walk through the woods. Ruben begins to share some valuable information with Ridge. Ruben tells Ridge that he knows his parents. Ridge inquires if Ruben had met his parents in the family store during his visit. Ruben looks at Ridge with a smile on his face and says, "It is very ironic that you would ask me how I know your parents." Ruben went on to say, "It is remarkably interesting how I am affiliated with your parents. You see, it is a little complicated, but I would just tell you that I know your parents from their past jobs. Ridge had no idea what his parents had done for a living in the past. Ridge is only aware of his parents' current occupations.

Jewel worked as a chemical engineer, and his father started and operated the family business that they now run together. Ruben's smile quickly turns into an upside-down frown as he starts to explain, "Well, you see, as I mentioned earlier, it is a bit of a complicated story. Unlike you and your brother, I did not have the pleasure of growing up with my parents; they were both taken from me at an early age. Family members raised me and even placed me in an orphanage a few times. You see, my father was a police officer who worked with the league. When he decided that he no longer wanted anything else to do with the league, he was killed. In the process of my father's demise, my mother, an innocent bystander, walked in, and she also was killed. Would you like to know who killed them?" Ruben asked again, "I SAID DO YOU WANNA KNOW!?" "YES! Yes, I do want to know," responds Ridge. "They were both killed by your mother, who was paid to do so." "MY MOTHER! Is this some kind of sick joke? I do not find it funny," Ridge angrily responded. "Do I look like I am laughing?" Ruben asked.

Ruben informs Ridge there has been a change in plans. Ridge, my son, instead of you hunting, you will be the one that is hunted.

Ridge begins to run as Ruben pulls out a gun and begins firing shots at him. Ridge returns fire, striking Ruben in the abdomen, and Ruben falls to the ground where he lays as he struggles to catch his breath. In his last minutes of life, Ruben vows to Ridge that he will stop at nothing until he kills Ridge's mother starting with Ridge. Ruben also tells Ridge that he should trust no one because the ones closest to him are the ones planning to kill him. Ruben points the gun at Ridge, and Ridge feels he has no choice but to finish Ruben. Ridge shoots Ruben again, striking him in the head and killing him instantly.

Ridge was shaken and saddened by the tragic event that unfolded but oddly got a rush; he felt the same way he did the first time he went hunting and killed his first prey. After the incident, Ridge reached out to Edge to share with him the events surrounding the tragedy. Oddly, before he could explain to Edge what happened, Edge responded that he would be there shortly. Not allowing Ridge to give him any details as to what happened or his true location. Edge arrives shortly and helps Ridge to hide Ruben's body.

Edge and Ridge turned and left the woods immediately after burying the corpse.

Stunned by what had taken place, they immediately went to see their parents to confront them about the information that Ruben had provided. Jewel confessed to killing Ruben's parents because Ruben's father was a disloyal member of the Justice League, and he was secretly working undercover to take down the league. Jewel revealed to them that she and Rellik were involved with the Justice League before giving birth to him and his brother. Jewel explained that their involvement was only a means of earning a living.

Jewel explains that the penalty for disloyal members of the Justice League is an automatic death sentence. She explained that Ruben's father had to be stopped, but in the process of his demise, his girlfriend walked in and saw Ruben's father's lifeless body lying on the floor. She was forced to kill Ruben's mother to keep her cover from being blown. As Jewel explains, Rellik quickly interrupts her. Rellik tells Jewel that she is missing the bigger picture. Rellik informs Jewel that now there is a bigger issue at hand.

The Love Triangle

Rellik wants to know who told Ruben that Jewel was the person that assassinated both of his parents and how they got that information. Prior to performing the hit, Jewel ensured that no one else was present except herself and the victim(s). The only other person that could have known about the incident was Collin, the CEO of the Justice League, because he is the one that is responsible for ordering and confirming all the hits. All hits remained confidential and held with the highest regard. Jewel and Rellik had not been in contact with the Justice League since Jewel declined the job to assassinate Rellik a few years earlier. The El'Poeps felt as if they were left with no option but to reach out to Collin and pose questions about the confidentiality of Jewel's hit on Ruben's parents. The El'Poeps set up a private meeting with Collin, but he refused to meet with them unless Ridge was present in the meeting, never requesting for Edge. Upon meeting with Collin, the Justice League's CEO, he promptly informed them that he had witnessed it. Ridge hunting on numerous occasions, and he noticed that

Ridge possesses many of his parents' characteristics and knows that Ridge would make an excellent assassin, just as both of his parents. He knows that if given a chance, Ridge has many hidden talents and needs help bringing them forth. He stated that he knew that Ruben had always wanted to know what happened to his parents, and telling Ruben about his parents was a test to see if Ruben had what it took to be an assassin. He explained that he had hoped that no one would be killed because he wanted to work with both Ruben and Ridge, but he knew that it would be likely that one man would not make it. He contends that the best man won. Jewel and Rellik became increasingly upset after hearing this information. Jewel began yelling, "YOU INTENTIONALLY SET UP OUR SON AND PUT OUR FAMILY IN DANGER FOR YOUR VERY OWN GAIN, AND NOW THAT HE HAS SURVIVED, YOU WANT HIM TO WORK FOR YOU!!!!" Collin responds, "Jewel, my dear, calm down. Once you are an assassin, you are always an assassin at heart. Jewel, my dear, you know the old saying that what does not kill you makes you stronger. I never even doubted once that you and your family would not be able to protect yourselves."

Collin tells them that Ridge came highly recommended by one of their newest and most trusted members, Edge. Rellik and Jewel came to learn that Edge had joined the Justice League some months earlier. Collin tells them that he promises to give Ridge a very generous contribution for his trouble. He also tells them he will also make sure that Ruben's remains are never found. Lastly, he promises them he will ensure that Rellik and Jewel are comfortable for the rest of their days on Earth. Collin provides training to Ridge and oversees that Ridge gets everything he needs to be comfortable.

Ridge, with the influence of Edge, decided against Jewel's wishes to join the Justice League. Ridge's life would change overnight. The League immediately sent Ridge out of the State to a remote island for training. Ridge trained for three months continuously, after which he was given his first assignment. Ridge's first assignment was his most difficult one. It was designed to assess his skills to find out if he was truly fit to be an assassin. Ridge's first assignment was to assassinate five drug lords that were imprisoned. Ridge had to not only go to prison but to a maximum-security prison to perform the hits.

The Alliance

The hits he performed were extremely risky because he could not trust anyone for fear of information being leaked. He never got the opportunity to meet the person that the League assigned to supply him with weapons. Different individuals gave him written instructions that told him where to go during certain times. During Ridge's imprisonment, a large brawl broke out among some rival gangs who were inmates. Ridge was caught in the crossfire, where he suffered a broken jaw and a serious head injury during the fight among the inmates. As a result of Ridge's head trauma, he found himself fighting with multiple personalities. There was Ridge, the hunter/assassin, followed by Richland, the businessman, and lastly, Robbie, the little boy who looked for love and affection. Robbie longed for love and affection and did not handle rejection of any type very well. While imprisoned, Ridge encountered a young woman by the name of Paige. Paige was from the opposite side of the tracks. Unlike Ridge, she grew up in an orphanage and never knew who her parents were or if she had any siblings. Everything that Paige was ever taught, she learned in the orphanage or on the streets of Brooklyn, New York.

Paige never had a job making an honest living; she had hustled, robbed, and conned people for the things that she had, which was not very much. Although Paige did not have very much, what she had meant a lot to her because she had never had anything she could call her very own. Growing up in an orphanage, she had to share everything she had with others. Paige's orphanage family meant a lot to her because they were the only family she had ever known. Paige got Ridge's attention in all the right ways. However, Paige was not very fond of Ridge because he was not her type. Paige liked men that were tall, physically fit, charming, adventurous, and were protective. Ridge, on the other hand, was the opposite. He was 5'6, and Paige was 5'5, barely taller than Paige. He was skinny, quiet, nerdy, and looked silly. Paige's feelings for Ridge would instantly change. One day, while on kitchen duty, Ridge overheard some female inmates plotting to kill Paige. Ridge immediately warned Paige while devising a plan to come to her rescue afterward, and they formed a bond that was unbreakable. The day had finally come for Ridge to be released after he had successfully performed all the hits that he was assigned to do, and just as the

Justice League had promised, they pulled some strings to make sure that he was released to go back to life, as he once knew it. Ridge refused to leave Paige behind; he insisted that the Justice League help her to get an early parole. Collin agreed to help Paige provided she became an active member of the League. After being released from prison, Ridge was given his next assignment by the League, and Paige was taken into training to become an assassin. When she completed her training, she was given her very first assignment. Paige's assignment was to assassinate the wife of a local mobster. She was given all the details that she needed to be able to pull off a successful hit. She was provided the tools to perform the assassination. She was told what she should wear and where she should go but was still unable to conduct the hit. Paige had committed many crimes in her life; conned people, robbed, and lied, but murder was not one that she could commit. Paige got dressed and entered the residence as planned, but upon entering the room where the mobster's wife stood, Paige contemplated leaving the room before the woman saw her and questioned her presence.

Paige stood contemplating her next move when she noticed the woman standing on the balcony of the high rise. Paige overhears the woman talking to herself. The woman sobs as she weights the pros and cons of her life. When the mobster's wife turns and spots Paige, she tells Paige about the problems she faces that have driven her to attempt suicide. The lady tells Paige that she and her high school love, who is now her husband, have been together for fifteen years, and they have been married for ten years. They have been trying to have kids for ten of the fifteen years and have been unsuccessful. She has just learned that her husband, a mobster, and drug kingpin, has been cheating on her for the last five years of their marriage. She had also learned that her husband and his mistress were expecting their second child, with the oldest being five years old. She tells Paige that she cannot withstand the pressure that comes along with living the life of a mobster's wife any longer. Paige pleaded with her as she witnessed the young woman jumping over the balcony of the high rise to her death. In disbelief by what she witnessed, Paige turned and ran.

Paige was reluctant to tell Collin for fear of her very own life. Paige lied to him about performing the hit. Upon returning and informing him that the hit was completed, he decided that since she was doing extremely well, he would assign her another hit. Paige's second assignment was to perform a hit on a crooked attorney. He failed to uphold a promise to oversee that a criminal case concerning one of the League's members was dismissed. The mobster was trialed and found guilty and sentenced to 30 years in prison. Paige was contracted to conduct a hit on the attorney. She was given a suitcase of supplies which contained a vanilla envelope to oversee what would be her second hit. The envelope contained details such as what time she was expected to arrive and the best entrance and exit points. Included in the suitcase was the outfit that should be worn during the hit, along with items to clean up afterward and the weapons to execute the hit. She was taught in training not to ever make eye contact with the victim and to quickly perform the hit without thinking about it twice. She was told to think of the victim as her worst enemy because if the hit is not a success, the victim could indeed be her worst enemy.

Paige had managed to escape her first hit but had no clues as to how she would avoid performing what was supposed to be her second, and she hoped it would be her final hit. The hit was scheduled to be performed at 6:00 am the following morning as the attorney left his residence on the way to his office. Paige knew that she had to perform the hit or devise an alternate plan quickly. Paige feared that if she did not perform the hit, her life could possibly be put in danger. Paige knew too much about the plot to assassinate the attorney and the Justice League to back out. Paige contemplated getting Ridge to perform the hit because he was indeed a professional assassin. There was just one problem; Ridge was out of town working an assignment and was not scheduled to return until the following week.

Later that evening, Paige got an unexpected phone call from Collin, the CEO of the League, to set up a meeting with her. He informed Paige that it was urgent that he spoke to her regarding some pressing issues of her first assignment. He informed her that he needed to speak with her prior to her hit the following morning. He arranged a meeting between himself and Paige for the following morning at 5:00 am.

Paige nervously walked the floor several times throughout the course of the night. She contemplated if she should go to the meeting with the CEO or pack her bags and leave town, never to look back ever again. If the League should ever find out the truth surrounding Paige's first hit, she would be assassinated for her dishonesty.

Early the following morning, Paige received a reminder call from Collin's secretary to confirm her meeting. After much debate, Paige decided that she was going to the meeting with Collin to see what he had to say. Upon leaving her residence and getting into her car, she immediately noticed a car tailing her. Paige immediately realized that she had made the right decision to attend the meeting the CEO had set up for her.

Paige arrived at the Justice League's headquarters for her meeting with Collin. As he learned of her arrival, he immediately called her into his office. Collin told Paige that he had been with the League for several years now and had encountered many types of people. From personal experience, he learned how to read and interpret a person's appearance and overall demeanor as to what type of agent a person will become.

He tells Paige that he knows that she is not a killer. Paige sits in silence as she looks on, her jaw drops. He explains to Paige that a new agent is never left completely alone on his or her first assignment and that there is always a veteran agent close by looking on to ensure that everything goes as planned. He then begins to explain to Paige that on the day of her assignment, due to a shortage of agents, he was the agent that looked on to ensure that everything went as planned with her assignment. He informs Paige that he witnessed the mobster's wife as she jumped to her death over the balcony. He tells Paige that he knew from their first meeting that being an assassin was not for her, but he wanted to help his fellow League members.

After hearing the news, Paige pulled herself together and asked Collin in an exceptionally low, soft voice, "Are you going to kill me?" Collin says, "Well, let me see; you have lied about the assignment in question, you have made an attempt to run, you have wasted the League's time, and lastly, you now have some valuable information that can destroy the entire Justice League. What do you think I should do to you?" He then tells her, "I will not kill you, at least this time, but you better never mumble a word of any of this to anyone ever."

Collin began telling Paige that he, too, had never killed anyone, and no one never knew about it except now Paige. He explained to Paige that his job was only to contract hits and verify that each hit was successfully carried out.

Soon afterwards, Collin and Paige began spending more time together, sharing more secrets, and eventually discovering that they had more in common than they could have ever imagined. Paige would soon learn that Collin had been an orphan at the same orphanage she lived. A family had adopted him a few months before Paige's arrival at the orphanage. They both were natives of Brooklyn, New York. They both encountered some of the very same people growing up but, oddly enough, had never encountered one another. A love affair would soon develop between Paige and the CEO; they were inseparable. It was as if Paige and the CEO had always known one another, and they complimented each other. They shared even their darkest secrets and most intimate moments with one another. He was everything that Paige had ever dreamed of, and they were madly in love. However, there was just one problem that stood in the way.

Ridge was officially Paige's boyfriend and was scheduled to be home from his 6-month assignment. Ridge was madly in love with Paige and planned to make her his wife. Upon Ridge's return, Paige tried to pick up where they left off, but her feelings for Ridge were not quite the same. Ridge could not physically or mentally please her like Collin was capable of satisfying her. Paige constantly found herself thinking about, wanting to be with, and longing for Collin's touch. Collin continued to find and send Ridge on assignments that took him far away from Paige. His assignments would last for days or even months. Paige decided that she wanted to be with Collin, so she decided to tell Ridge that she needed them to take a break from one another. Ridge questioned Paige's reasoning for her decision to end their relationship. Paige was Ridge's first girlfriend, and he loved her with all his heart. Ridge was devastated by the breakup and vowed to fight until the end to win her back. Ridge could not sleep and refused to eat for days. Ridge turned into Robbie, who could not deal with Paige's refusal. Robbie demanded to have an answer from Paige.

Robbie began snooping and following Paige, and he would soon learn of Paige's involvement with Collin. Robbie began acting out. Robbie broke into Paige's home, where he hid in the closet waiting for her arrival. Paige arrived sometime later, accompanied by her now boyfriend Collin. As Paige and Collin settle in for the remainder of the night in preparation for an early morning, Robbie surprises them. They are awakened by Robbie as he stood at the foot of the bed weeping uncontrollably and yelling, "Liar!" "Liar!" "Liar!" Paige runs out of the house as Collin runs behind her. Robbie corners Paige as he quickly pulls out his knife and begins stabbing her. In Robbie's mind, he thinks that he is stabbing Collin, only to find out as he switches back to Ridge that he has stabbed his one and only love, Paige. Ridge immediately grabs her as he apologizes for his actions and begs her not to die. Paige's body can be seen slumped over on the ground as her clothes became quickly saturated with her very own blood. In her last moments of life, she tells Ridge that she forgives him and that it was all her fault. Paige makes Ridge promise that he will not kill or retaliate in any way on Collin. Ridge promises Paige that he will not kill or harm Collin in any way.

Paige closes her eyes, taking her very last breath. Paige succumbed to her injuries as she had lost a significant amount of blood. Collin is unable to deal with losing the love of his life, his soul mate, Paige. Ridge looks up to find himself looking down the barrel of Collin's gun. Collin tells Ridge, "You may have promised not to kill me, but I never promised that I wouldn't kill you for killing my beloved Paige." Before Collin could pull the trigger, Ridge is shot from behind by his very own brother, Edge. Jewel, "Head-Hunter," began searching for answers surrounding Ridge's death. When Collin is confronted with the circumstances surrounding Ridge's death, Jewel learns some life-changing details surrounding Ridge's murder that will impact the way she views her family. Jewel soon learns of a nearby camera that may have captured the events leading up to Ridge's death. Upon watching the video, she learns that Collin was not the killer, but it was her very own beloved Edge that killed Ridge. Ridge's autopsy results later confirmed that the bullet that killed Ridge was fired from Edge's gun that he nicked named "Do Something." Jewel, "Head-Hunter," learned that Rellik also played a role in the murder of their son Ridge.

Jewel, "Head-Hunter," would later come to learn that Rellik had contracted a hit on his very own son. Collin finally admits that he was asked to kill Ridge because he was an embarrassment to Rellik. Ridge suffered from multiple personalities due to a head trauma sustained in prison which Rellik felt diminished his quality of life. When Collin was unable to perform the hit, Edge stepped in to prove his loyalty to his father and the organization, which all made sense when Ridge told Hunter that prior to Ruben's death, he was warned to watch the ones that were closest to him.

When confronted by Jewel, "Head-Hunter," Rellik denied all accusations. Jewel mourned Ridge's death. Jewel, "Head-Hunter," upon learning of Rellik's involvement, felt she could no longer trust him, so she decided to end their marriage by filing for a divorce. Jewel immediately left town, cutting off all ties with Rellik and Edge. Jewel, being an assassin, knew all too well how to conceal her identity. Rellik looked for her, but there was no sign of her anywhere; her where abouts remained unknown.

Chapter 4:

The Ultimate Betrayal

Edge's Fling

Eighteen years later, Rellik, Edge, and Collin have now joined forces to form a new and revised New World Order Justice League. They play by no rules; any and everything goes. Edge advises a plan to get rid of Rellik and Collin in an attempt to take over the league. Edge takes an assignment to assassinate a local politician where he plans to set up Rellik and Collin as accessories for the murder for hire. Edge's plan is to get both Collin and Rellik out of the picture so that he may have complete control over the New World Order Justice League. The New World Order Justice League brought in millions of dollars for them. The League was the first of its kind; it consisted of murder, money laundering, drug trafficking, as well as human trafficking.

The League had changed a lot from when Rellik and Hunter first joined years earlier. The Justice League, when Rellik and Hunter first became members, had dignity and honor despite the type of work that was performed. In the New World Order, it was a dog-eat-dog world. Edge is hired to assassinate the Senator. Edge attends an electoral party where he plans to assassinate Senator Rodney Holleman. At the event, he meets and immediately falls head over heels for the hostess of the event. She was tall and thin with curves in all the right places. She was a goddess that commanded attention to her presents. She was not only beautiful but charming and smart and knew all the right things to say. She knew how to work a room. She showed pause and grace in her every move. She was the center of attention.

She was who every woman dreamed of becoming and every man's desire. Edge and the hostess had an instant connection as if they were meant for one another. Their chemistry was undeniable. As their eyes locked, it became obvious that it was love at first sight. They immediately hit it off as if they were meant to be. Who was this mystery lady, and where had she been? Edge eagerly waits for her to become available; nervously, he asks her to dance.

Before Edge could finish his sentence, she immediately cuts him off, answering "yes." Edge interjects with a smile on his face, "but you don't know what I was about to ask you." She smiles and says, "It's still a yes for me." Edge and the mystery lady dance as he is visibly shaken and overtaken by her beauty.

Edge never believed in love at first sight until now. He looked into her eyes and knew there was something special about her. Edge knew that he had to have her. Edge is finally able to pull himself together to introduce himself. "Hello, my name is Edge. And beautiful, what might your name be?" She then introduced herself to Edge, "Hi, I am District Attorney Nalerie Hollerman." Edge repeats, "Hollerman?" "Yes, I am the daughter of Senator Hollerman." Edge stood in silence.

Edge was there to assassinate Senator Rodney Hollerman, and his daughter now happened to be the most beautiful lady that he had ever laid eyes on. Not only was she the senator's daughter, but she was also the head criminal prosecutor of the district. "Is something wrong?" She asked. "No, I just never knew that Senator Hollerman had such a beautiful daughter." Edge and Nalerie were inseparable; they danced the rest of the evening.

As they danced, Edge thought about how much he wanted to get to know Nalerie on a more personal level. Edge wondered what would happen if she ever learned the real reason, he was attending the electoral party was to assassinate her father.

Edge had never let anyone come in between his job and the opportunity to make a grand. This time, things were different more than anything; he wanted to get to know Nalerie. He hoped that their friendship could turn into a meaningful relationship. Edge was certain that she was the love of his life. If she ever found out his reason for attending the event, he would not have a fighting chance to be with Nalerie; their relationship would be over before it even got started. The assignment must be completed because the job has already been paid for in advance. Edge contemplated giving the job to Collin because it would make it easier to set Collin up if he performed the job for hire. Edge would then only have to devise a plan to get rid of Rellik so that he can be the new CEO of the New World Order Justice League. Edge wanted to make sure that all evidence led back to Collin. Collin would be identified as the killer. Edge could not risk Rellik finding out his plan to destroy him and Collin.

Edge, more than anyone else, knew how dangerous his father had the potential to be. Edge reached out to an old colleague who was a member of the original Justice League to put him in contact with a member that could carry out the hit. Edge decided to choose a beautiful female decoy. The hired assassin was a new member of the Justice League. Edge wanted to get someone that could lower him in and gain the trust of Senator Rodney Hollerman. The person for hire went by the name of Jae, "The Dream-killer." Upon Edge meeting "The Dream-killer," it was as if she, in some ways, reminded him of himself, and he felt as if he had already known her. Edge and "The Dream-killer" thought a lot alike. Edge and Jae, "The Dream-killer," instantly became friends. Edge was older than her, but she was wise beyond her years.

Although "The Dream-killer" was new to the League, she was a "blood-born assassin." She had a niche for what she did, made no mistakes, and challenged anyone who questioned or got in her way. Meanwhile, Edge and Nalerie's relationship continued to blossom. Edge and Nalerie became exclusive almost overnight. They fell madly in love.

Edge fell head over heels in love with Nalerie as he would ultimately let his guard down. Nalerie's curiosity got the best of her, and she began secretly investigating Edge. Nalerie began snooping through Edge's personal items.

One morning, before leaving Edge's home after a night of hot passionate lovemaking, she ran across some important documents of Edge. The documents contained the contract that detailed the plot and agreement to kill Nalerie's father, the senator. Nalerie brought it to Edge's attention the following night over dinner at her house. "Edge, my love, and you are my love? Could you please explain to me the proposed plan surrounding the documents in this folder?"

Edge opened the envelope and began viewing the documents; he immediately realized that they were the documents from his library. Clearly, she must have been going through his files to have found the original contract to kill her father. Edge feared that this would mark the end of their relationship, as he even feared the worst of having to kill the love of his life. He had finally found the love of his life, his soulmate. He did not want to have to kill her for the sake of her blowing the case.

Edge began to try to convince his beloved Nalerie of his innocence. Nalerie immediately cut him off. "I see that this is a ridiculously small world. The best league of assassins bought this contract; they are the Newly Formed Justice League, so please tell me how you got it?"

Edge was surprised by what he had just heard. He stares at her for a second as he gathers his thoughts. Edge asks her if she would please repeat what she has just said. She promptly informs him that he heard her correctly. Edge asks Nalerie if she is involved in the plot to end her father's life. She tells him that she is the mastermind behind the hit on her father. She tells Edge how her father was very abusive to her, her mother, and several other members of their family growing up as a child and how he must be stopped.

She tells Edge about the horrible things that her father does daily to people, and he must not be allowed to continue to hurt people. She tells Edge that her father also suffers from mental illness.

Edge admits to Nalerie that he was the contracted assassin to kill her father, but after meeting her, he has since decided to give the contract to another contractor who happened to be a female decoy to lower and kill the senator.

Nalerie tells Edge that she would like to quickly assassinate her father because she feels that society is not safe as long as he is still alive. But what Edge does not know is that Nalerie has a gambling debt and plans to use Hollerman's life insurance policy to pay off her debt. Nalerie asks Edge to reconsider taking on the case again to expedite the process.

Jae, "The Dream-killer," began working on a plan to assassinate the senator. "The Dream-killer" began following the senator very closely, which made it difficult. The senator's schedule was unpredictable because he was truly a family-oriented person and was always surrounded by loved ones and friends. The only thing that remained the same was his church and bible study schedules. "The Dream-killer" was running out of time as it was an urgent job for hire.

She was running out of ways to try to lower the senator. He was always in church or in the company of other family members, mainly young children. During "The Dream-killer" research, she came to learn that the young children were the senator's grandchildren. "The Dream-killer" discovered that the senator had an older daughter other than Nalerie, who was the children's mother.

"The Dream-killer" learned that the senator's older daughter was currently living in a mental health facility in a city twelve hours away. When asked about her sister, Nalerie told Edge that she had no idea of her sister's whereabouts. Nalerie explained that her sister, just like her father suffered from mental illness. She told Edge that it was not unusual for her sister to go missing for months at a time. Her whereabout remain unknown as she requested never to have the family involved in her life again. "The Dream-killer" and Edge decided to visit Bella Hollerman, Nalerie's sister. They visited the mental health facility to get more information. Edge was hoping to surprise Nalerie with her sister's whereabouts. However, Edge was indeed the one that was in for a surprise. Upon meeting Bella, Edge introduces himself as a friend of Nalerie. Bella immediately becomes upset by Edge's presence, stating that she was drugged and brought to the facility against her will by Nalerie. Bella maintains that there is nothing wrong with her. Bella tells Edge that Nalerie is a spoiled brat and just wants to get her out of the way.

Bella tells Edge that Nalerie is extremely dangerous and cannot be trusted, and she is only looking out for herself. Bella tells Edge that Nalerie has produced a plan to get rid of her and their parents so that she can take over the family's business and get her inheritance. Bella insists that she is not mentally unstable and is very aware of her sister's intentions. She begs Edge for help to get out of the asylum so she can get back to her life. She tells him how she misses her children dearly. Bella warns Edge that if he utters a word of his visit to Nalerie, she will have her moved to a different facility or, even worse, possibly killed. Edge promises Bella that if she is honest with him, he will make sure that she gets out of the mental health institution and is reunited with her children. Edge asks her to give him some time to advise on a plan to get her out of the mental health institution. Jae, "The Dream-killer," continues to follow and investigates Senator Hollerman. As she investigates Senator Hollerman, she grows fond of him. Jae, "The Dream-killer," soon sees the type of person Senator Hollerman really is, and she is pleasantly surprised. Senator Hollerman was not the monster that she had envisioned. In fact, he was the total opposite.

The senator was the type of man that helped any and everyone in any way possible. His love for children was undeniable. He was highly active in his church and took on many roles in the community. "The Dream-killer" could not understand why any sane person would want to kill the senator. "The Dream-killer" was still new to the league, but she had completed more than ten assassinations during her twelve-month period with the League. "The Dream-killer" had no problem ever performing an assassination on anyone. However, this one was different. "The Dream-killer" could not see herself killing the senator because he was one of the nicest men she had ever met, which made it extremely difficult to dislike him, not to mention kill him. It became clear to her that this was an obvious mistake.

They began to wonder if what Bella said about Nalerie was true. Nalerie was very evil, cold-blooded, manipulative, and spoiled, and perhaps placed the hit on her very own parents for her financial gain. Jae, "The Dream-killer," went out of her way to purposely meet the senator. She wanted to converse with him to see if he really and truly was as innocent and nice of a guy as he appeared outwardly. As much as Jae,

"The Dream-killer," hated to do it, she decided to attend church service at the senator's church to be able to speak to him. The senator was very welcoming to her, not knowing her true objectives for attending the service. He welcomed her with open arms as she continued to attend the church's services to get more information about the senator. During her visits to the senator's church, she began to become interested in the services. It was as if the preacher was speaking to her. She could not understand because he did not know her or any problems that she would be facing. A feeling came over her that was unexplainable. It was a feeling that was unfamiliar to her. It was a feeling of peace, one of love and final acceptance. It was a feeling that she had never experienced before but one that she never wanted to lose. It was a feeling that no words in the English language could effectively describe. She desired to learn more. Jae, "The Dream-killer," continued to visit the Hollermans church until finally deciding to accept the invitation to join the church and accepting God as her personal savior. The senator would ultimately invite her to dinner at the family's home. He treated her from day one as if she were one of his daughters.

The senator would hold bible studies at his home for the members of his church. Jae found herself before long attending bible studies. Jae and the Hollermans became the best of friends. Jae began to look at him as a father figure. She began to question her purpose in life. Jae's character transitioned for the better. She knew that she had to leave the League. She no longer wanted to work for the League. She repented for her sins and no longer wanted to be associated with the League, let alone be called "The Dream-killer." Now she is "The Dream-builder" for Christ. She began studying the bible more; she wanted a better understanding of the bible and how it related to her very own existence. In everything that she did, she sorted to please Christ. Jae was a woman after Christ's own heart. Jae, Mr., and Mrs. Hollerman began to embark on a relationship that she would never have imagined in her wildest dream.

Meanwhile, Nalerie began to constantly fight with Edge as she questioned why the senator had not been assassinated. Nalerie contends that he is very evil and has hurt many innocent people and that he must be stopped.

Nalerie tells Edge that she will get someone else if he cannot be man enough to do the job. Jae tells Edge that not only will she not kill senator Hollerman, but she also no longer works for the League and does not want anything else to do with the League or its dealings. Jae tells Edge that if he wants the senator killed, he either must do it himself or get someone else to do the job. Jae urges Edge to get to know the senator first before following through on his plan. Jae and Edge began to think that Bella was right. Jae tells Edge that Mr. and Mrs. Hollerman are convinced that Bella abandoned her children. The Hollermans are not aware that Bella was drugged and put in a mental institution against her will. Jae and Edge came up with a plan to get Bella out of the mental institution. For this plan to be effective, they must tell the Hollermans everything that Nalerie has done, from the murder plot to the lies and constant manipulation. Edge knows that he must decide to either help the Hollermans or be on Nalerie's side. Edge is aware that, ultimately, he and Nalerie's relationship is going to end once he helps Bella and the Hollermans.

Edge tells Nalerie that he knows about her plan to kill her father so she can get her inheritance and the life insurance policy. The life insurance states that if anything should happen to him, his wife, and Bella, everything would be left to Nalerie. Nalerie would stand to inherit everything the Hollermans own over billions of dollars of assets. Nalerie surprisingly does not deny Edge's allegations, but she admits to Edge that he is much smarter than she had given him credit. Nalerie tells Edge that they are more alike than he thought. The stakes are now higher, and Nalerie is running out of time. Nalerie threatens Edge to help her to kill her family, which now includes her mother and sister, or she will reveal the real reason he initially took the contract in the beginning. Nalerie laughs, telling Edge that she is extremely disappointed in him. She assures Edge that if it should ever get out about her involvement in her parent's death, not only does she have a lot on the line, but she is also the state's head district attorney. Nalerie threatens Edge, "you will surely be killed if your father, who is a mafia boss, finds out how you had planned to portray him to steal the business that he built."

However, it would be even more interesting if your organization were finally caught and charged for the numerous murders that you all have committed. You, my love, your father, and your business partner will never again see the light of day. Now, do you think that you want that on your hands?" Edge looks on in disgust. Nalerie continues, "I do not think you wanted to deal with that. I want to also remind you, my love, that I am the chief judge, so I have the power to make some things happen." Edge cuts in, saying, "you know, now I realize there is one thing that is different about us. If I were indicted for my crime, I would survive. In fact, I would be held in high regard. However, if you, on the other hand, were indicted, would you survive? Everyone knows that you are on the opposite side of the law; in fact, you were the cause of many people losing their freedom. I will give you a minute to think about that answer, my dear." As he smirks and walks away, Nalerie comments as she raises a glass of wine, "my dear, it looks like we both have our work cut out for us; may the best man or woman wins." Nalerie and Edge's relationship is bittersweet.

Edge is forced to follow through with the plot to kill the senator, but now the stakes are higher. There is more money involved, which now includes the assassination of the senator's wife, Nalerie's stepmother, and her sister Bella. Collin is given the job.

The Hit

Collin is preparing to perform the hit when he gets a lead from an informant that the Hollermans had planned a trip to Paris. He plans to have them assassinated when they arrive in Paris because they would be away from their grandchildren and other family members and friends. Collin finds out that Mr. and Mrs. Hollerman have landed in Paris and are being escorted to their rooms. When given the signal, they will be assassinated in their rooms, making sure not to leave any witnesses. Collin decided to pass the hit off to a newly recruited assassin of the League. It would be his first hit and initiation into the League, allowing him to prove himself as a trusting member. When Collin got the call, he immediately summoned the new agent, "The Destroyer," to execute the Hollermans.

Everything went as planned. Collin later got a confirmation call saying that the hit had been successful. Collin immediately phoned Edge to say that the hit was a success. Edge then reached out to Nalerie and left her a voicemail message on her phone to inform her that the hit had been carried out on her parents, as she had requested.

Edge reached out to Jae to give her his condolences because he knew how fond of the Hollermans she had become.

Jae called Edge back to inform him that she had been with the Hollermans most of the morning and had just left them at their Malibu home. Clearly, there must have been a mistake because the Hollermans were not in Paris. Edge immediately reached out to the contractor "The Destroyer" to get confirmation pictures of the victims that were assassinated. In the pictures that Edge retrieved was a picture of a dark head gentleman who was later identified as Nalerie's co-worker, and the final picture was that of none other than Nalerie Hollerman. It was rumored that the two had been a couple for two years off and on. It was later discovered that the man was married with two children.

The man and Nalerie had checked into a luxury hotel in Paris as Mr. and Mrs. Hollerman in an attempt to hide the man's identity. Edge was saddened by the events that took place and to discover that the love of his life had been seeking the attention of another. Edge felt a sense of relief knowing that he no longer had to feel threatened by Nalerie to expose his plan. Edge's relief would not last long; it would be short-lived.

The Setup

A few weeks later, Edge received a visit from the local authorities to arrest him for his role in the murder plot of the Hollermans. Edge's very own confession, which was heard on Nalerie's voicemail during the investigation of her death, was enough to arrest Edge. Edge could not believe what he was hearing. The police were escorted by Rellik and Collin, who both got word that Edge was planning to set them up for the murders. Collin's decoy Christopher, "The Destroyer," had been instructed to set up Edge for the murders.

The police heard Edge's voicemail left on Nalerie's phone, showing that he had planned to kill her parents, and they believed that when he learned of her cheating, he decided to kill her and her lover instead.

Edge stares at Rellik and Collin in total disbelief as he is read his rights and placed in police custody. Edge vows to destroy Rellik and Collin at all costs if it is the last thing that he does. Bella is released from the asylum and allowed to return to her life before her sister abruptly interrupts it. Jae explains everything to the Hollermans as they sit in disbelief after learning the truth about Nalerie.

The Hollermans decided to honor Nalerie with a lovely homegoing celebration but refused to be in attendance for the celebration. Thank you, cards were sent to all that attended the celebration.

Chapter 5:

The Wedding

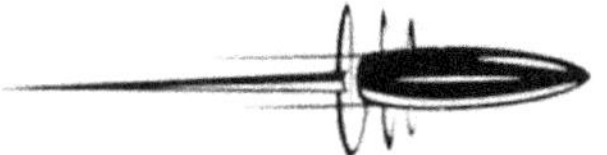

Murder for Hire

The new assassin Christopher "The Destroyer," as he came to be known, completed the hit and was initiated into the New World Order Justice League, where he would take Edge's place. "The Destroyer" was always confident in his abilities to carry out hits. He felt as if he did not need anyone else and that he was more than enough. Christopher "The Destroyer" performed twenty more hits by himself in addition to the initial hit in the assassination of Nalerie Hollerman and her co-worker. "The Destroyer" became very arrogant and overly confident in himself.

"The Destroyer" and Jae, formerly "The Dream-killer," bumped heads constantly for "The Destroyer's" egotistic attitude.

They were like night and day. The only thing that they could agree on was to disagree. Jae despised him and hated being in his presence. In many instances, she wished she could kill him herself, free of charge, just so she would not have to see him again.

They argued every chance they got. Rellik assigned Jae an assassination to perform. Rellik asked Christopher, "The Destroyer," to go with Jae to oversee her with the job since it had been a while since she had performed a hit. Jae accepted the job against her better judgment because she desperately needed the money. All the details were given to her as to what she needed to do.

Upon arriving to complete the job, Jae could not pull the trigger, and the victim turned and began firing shots at her. She tripped and fell on the ground as she attempted to run. The victim stood over her, aiming the gun at Jae's head when Christopher, "The Destroyer," appeared out of nowhere. Christopher pulled the trigger shooting the gunman from behind and killing him. Jae was shaken by the events that unfolded before her very own eyes. In the car, Jae reflects on the event that could have ended her life.

She thanks "The Destroyer" for saving her life. "The Destroyer" asks Jae what happened and why she froze, unable to pull the trigger. Jae tried to explain as tears ran down her face. She explained to "The Destroyer" that something in her would not allow her to pull the trigger. She tells him that even though she does not understand, she has never experienced anything like it. It was almost the same feeling she got when she attended the Hollermans' church for the first time. Jae told "The Destroyer" that although she did not see him, she knew she would be all right. Jae's peace compasses all understanding and cannot be explained.

Jae told Rellik and Collin that she must leave the League effectively immediately. Jae requested never to be referred to as "The Dream-killer" again. Jae knew deep down inside that she did not have the power or authority to kill and steal anyone's life, let alone their dream. Jae immediately falls to her knees, where she repents for her sins and worships and praises God, who is in charge of everyone and everything.

Jae's life was forever changed. Jae was not sure how Rellik and the others would perceive her or how they would feel about her decisions.

She did not care; all she cared about was doing what was right and acceptable in the eyes of her Lord and savior. Nothing else mattered. She could still hear parts of the church sermon that had been preached at the Hollerman's church, which was now also her church, being recited in her head. Jae and Christopher, "The Destroyer," remained in contact even after she left the League. Jae was thankful to him for saving her life, as they would form a bond. They became the absolute best of friends. They began hanging out together. She invited him to go to church with her. One thing led to another, and they soon began dating. Christopher would soon ask for Jae's hand in marriage.

The New World Order Justice League (Rellik and Collin) decided to have an elaborate wedding for Christopher (The Destroyer) and Jae (formally The Dream-killer), followed by a honeymoon in Cuba. The New World Order Justice League figured that it would be fitting since the League bought the two together, but there was one catch to it all. "The Destroyer" is contracted to perform a hit while in Cuba on his honeymoon with Jae. He will not be made aware of the hit until arriving in Cuba.

The assassination is that of a celebrity who will also be visiting Cuba. The job is an extremely dangerous job, but they are certain that "The Destroyer" can pull it off without any problems. The big day has finally come for Christopher and Jae to confess their love for one another. Christopher and Jae had a lovely wedding full of surprises in a beautiful chapel overlooking the beach in Paris, France. One surprise that no one saw coming. Jae introduced her parents to Rellik and Collin. Rellik is speechless when he learns that Jae's mother is none other than his beloved Jewel. Rellik knew that Jae reminded him of someone that he knew, but it has now come crystal clear. Jae's mannerisms were a lot like Jewels. Rellik was astonished to find out that Jewel was remarried and had a daughter. Rellik was really surprised that Jae had been working for his organization for three years, and he never knew that she was Jewel's daughter. To make matters worse, Jae even helped Rellik put Edge (her brother) behind bars. Jewel was just as shocked to see Rellik as he was to see her. Jewel then figured out the line of work that her daughter was doing. Jae had always told Jewel that she worked in the Criminal Justice System. Jewel never figured in her wildest dreams that Jae, too, was an assassin.

Jewel tried to ensure that Jae's childhood was different from her brothers. Jewel's husband, Robert, Jae's father had no idea what was going on; he was completely in the dark about everything.

Robert knew what Jewel told him about her past. However, Jewel never revealed to him her past as an assassin. After the completion of Jae and Christopher's wedding ceremony, they boarded a private jet. They are flown to Cuba to start their honeymoon. Prior to landing in Cuba, Christopher, "The Destroyer," receives a phone call from Collin informing him of a job for hire effective immediately upon arrival. The job is one that "The Destroyer" cannot refuse because it is the highest paying hit he has ever had since joining the League. Christopher worried about what might happen if Jae found out about the job for hire. Christopher had promised her that he would not take any more jobs from the League in an effort to change his life. Christopher promised Jae that he would get a regular 9 to 5 job. As Jae is in the shower, Christopher contemplates the assassination plot, and he serves her an alcoholic drink. As Jae falls asleep, Christopher sneaks out of the room to carry out the assassination.

Christopher returned to the room an hour before daybreak and climbed into bed with Jae as she is still asleep.

At noon, Collin contacts Christopher to confirm that the hit was successfully completed, and Christopher reassures him that it went off without any major problems. Jae overhears him and immediately gets very angry with Christopher. Jae tells Christopher that it has not been 24 hours yet, and he has already violated one of the rules of their marriage.

Jae was upset that Rellik and Collin would give Christopher a hit on their honeymoon with no regard to the fact that they had just gotten married. Jae argued that Rellik and Collin intentionally sent them on a honeymoon to Cuba to be able to perform the hit. Jae storms out of the room and leaves the hotel.

Christopher calls Jae several times but only gets her voicemail, pleading with her to return to the hotel so that they can talk and work things out.

The Abduction

The following morning, there was still no sign of Jae. Christopher began to worry because Jae hadn't gotten this mad with him to the extent of not returning his phone call nor coming home. Christopher went out to look for Jae, but she was nowhere to be found. Christopher alerted Rellik and Collin back at home about Jae's disappearance. Rellik, Collin, Jewel, and Robert came to Cuba to help Christopher look for Jae. Three weeks passed before they learned that Jae had been abducted and was being held captive. They had suspected that something terrible had happened, but they never suspected that she was a victim of an underground human trafficking ring. Jae was unbelievably beautiful, and she was like the splitting image of her mother, Jewel, in her younger days. Jae's skin was olive, her bone structure was very prominent, she had high cheekbones and a smile that would melt your heart with a laugh that was infectious, and her eyes commanded your attention with long flowing hair. They began working around the clock to get Jae back. Jewel's true identity began to resurface.

Robert, Jae's father, wanted to contact the authorities for assistance with getting Jae back. Jewel, Rellik, Collin, and Christopher produced their own plan to get Jae back. Robert, an innocent retired engineer, had no idea that he was dealing with "blood-born assassins" and that killing was second nature to them. Robert had only ever owned one handgun, and it was only shot during its yearly testing on the fourth of July. Robert feared for Jewel's safety. He had possibly lost his daughter, and now he did not want to lose his wife. Robert insisted on participating in the search for Jae to ensure the safe return of his wife and daughter.

They formed two groups to look for Jae. Rellik and Collin went together, and Jewel, Christopher, and Robert were together. It would not be long before Robert learns Jewel's secret that she had worked so diligently trying to hide from him throughout the years of their marriage. The group gets word about where Jae is located. They storm in and open fire on the kidnappers where Jae is being held captive. Jae turns around just in time to see one of the kidnappers pointing his gun at Christopher. Jae pushes Christopher out of the way of the gunman, but Jae is hit by the stray bullet of the gun.

The bullet strikes her in the upper right quadrant of her chest. Christopher immediately fires back at the gunman, hitting him several times before Jewel fires the fatal shot to the head, killing him. Robert, Jewel's husband, witnesses it all and cannot believe his eyes. Robert is in shock as he stares at the lifeless body lying on the floor. Jewel, unbothered by the incident, yells to Collin and Rellik to help Christopher get Jae to safety for medical attention.

Jae's True Identity

When they arrived at the hospital, Jae had to be rushed into surgery immediately to save her life. Jae had lost a significant amount of blood. Jae's doctor told Jewel that if Jae's to pull through this ordeal, she would need some blood to survive. Jewel, without hesitation, agrees to donate some blood for Jae. The doctors got Jewel set up for the blood transfusion. It would not be long before Jewel was faced with yet another crisis. Jae's doctor requested to speak with Jewel informing her that Jae's blood type was rare, and as a result, her blood type did not match Jae's blood type. The doctor suggested that Robert Jae's father be crossed and typed to be the donor.

Jewel had type A-positive, and Jae had AB-negative. Jewel knew that Ridge, before his passing, had type AB-negative just as his father Rellik and Edge had his mother's blood type. Jewel cannot believe what she is hearing. Could Rellik be Jae's father instead of Robert, or does Robert also has AB-negative? Studies show that AB-negative is the rarest blood type in the United States, and only 1% of the population has that blood type.

As the doctor informs Jewel about Jae's blood type, she looks over at Robert. Robert looks at Jewel with his eyes filled with tears. Robert tells Jewel that his blood type is O-positive. Jewel looks at Rellik, who stands there in disbelief. The doctor tests Rellik and finds out that his blood type is a perfect match. Rellik's DNA sample indicated that he is Jae's biological father. Jewel stood in silence as she tried to understand how she could not have known that she was pregnant with Jae when she left Rellik. Jewel met Robert one month after leaving Rellik. It all began to make sense now to Robert. Jewel had never really talked to Robert about her past or what took place in her marriage that led to her getting divorced. Robert began to put it all together.

He was distraught over the events that had just unfolded in his presence. When everyone else, including his wife, who literally had just blown off someone's head, was unbothered by it all. Everyone, apart from himself, looked as if they were professionals when it came down to the operation of a gun and the order of arrangement of events. Robert began to think that this whole meeting was much bigger than himself or Jae's kidnapping.

Robert began questioning Jewel about the events that took place as well as her past life surrounding Rellik. Jewel had been out of the game for a while, but she knew how the League operated. If at any time the League felt as if an individual were a threat or would jeopardize the League, they would be commissioned to assassinate that individual. The League had far too much on the line to jeopardize it for just one person. Jewel really loved Robert and was very apologetic for the hurt and pain she had caused him. The last thing that she wanted to do was to bring harm to him. Jewel did not want to see Robert killed or hurt anymore (than he already had been) because of his genuine concern for her and their family.

Jewel was willing to go to any length to help Robert recover from the incident. She knew that it was far too tragic for him to ever just forget about the entire incident. Jewel came up with a plan to have Robert see a doctor when they returned to the states to help him cope with the tragedy.

When Jae was well enough to travel, they had her airlifted to the local hospital in their city for continued treatment. Robert and Jewel's communication was not as it was prior to their trip to Cuba. Jewel scheduled a therapy session for Robert. The therapist suggests that Jewel have Robert hypnotized to save their marriage. During the hypnosis, Robert would have no recollection of his trip to Cuba. Things would be just the way they were prior to going to Cuba. Jewel asks Rellik and the others not to tell Jae that Rellik is her biological father. She knew it would hurt Jae because she and Robert had a remarkably close father-and-daughter bond, not to mention that it would perhaps trigger Robert's memory of those events, opening old wounds for him. Against their better judgment, they all agreed to keep it a secret.

It was becoming increasingly difficult for Rellik to keep the secret that he was Jae's father. Jae is Rellik's first and only daughter.

He was overly excited and wanted the opportunity to be able to spoil her. Rellik liked Jae from the first day he met her. He saw a fighter in her. She seemed soft but had the ability to be tough as nails when it came down to business. Rellik wanted to get to know Jae on a more personal level. He had missed Jae's childhood, and now he wanted her to be in his life as much as humanly possible. Meanwhile, Jae thinks that Rellik is feeling sympathetic for his role in the incident that took place in Cuba, which almost caused her to lose her life.

Rellik began buying Jae and Christopher expensive presents. He buys Jae and Christopher a mini mansion in a gated community. Their home is furnished with the most expensive furnishing exported from Italy's finest furniture stores. Rellik buys them both the cars of their dreams.

Chapter 6:

Edge's Return

The Assault

Having almost lost her life, Jae is even now more grateful to her Lord and savior and vows to dedicate her time to help in the church. Jae becomes a mentor for the young girls in the church. Just as things are beginning to look up for Jae and Christopher, it takes a turn for the worst. Jae is home winding down and preparing for dinner when she gets a knock on the door. Jae opens the door and finds two police officers standing on her porch. Jae immediately senses that something is terribly wrong.

Jae feared that with her and Christopher's past with the New World Order Justice League that the police had finally caught up with them. The officer asked Jae if she was Christopher's wife. Jae asked the officers what was wrong.

They asked Jae if they could come in to speak with her. They ask Jae if she knows anyone Christopher is having trouble with that would like to see him dead. Jae says no and asks where her husband is. They informed her that Christopher's car had received multiple rounds of gunfire upon stopping at the red light, and he was struck multiple times and has been rushed to the hospital.

Jae rushed to the local hospital to be by her husband's side. Arriving at the hospital, Jae is not prepared for what she sees. Christopher is placed on life support, where he lies fighting for his life. Christopher was placed on a ventilator, with tubes running from both his mouth and nose, as the machine consistently pumped air in and out of his lungs. After seeing him, Jae feels as if someone has literally reached in and snatched out her heart. The pain she felt was unbearable. It was as if she was having a nightmare that was never-ending. Jae knew that he had a hand in the demise of many people; there could have been several people to blame.

Overwhelmed by it all, Jae fainted, and when she awoke, she found herself having been placed in a room in one of the hospital's beds, surrounded by Jewel, Rellik, and Robert.

The nurse that was assigned to oversee her told Jae that she had some good news that she hoped would enlighten her day. The nurse told Jae that she was currently eight weeks pregnant. Jae is overly excited that it will be their first child because she and Christopher have been trying to conceive for several months. Jewel, Rellik, and Robert are all overly excited about learning that they are going to be grandparents. Rellik vows to Jae that he will get the person responsible for the attack on Christopher. Rellik and Collin investigated to find out who was behind the attempted assassination of Christopher. They were one of the best in the business. If they could not find the perpetrators behind the incident, then no one could find them. Rellik quickly concluded that the leads were dead ends. Rellik demanded that Jae should focus on her family and allow himself and Collin to do the rest. Two months went by before they were able to take Christopher off the ventilator. Rellik and Collin still had no leads. Jae could not let the person that tried to kill Christopher get away with almost killing her husband, and she was determined to get revenge.

Jae had resigned from the League quite some time ago, rededicating her life back to God, but Jae had to get closure. Jae began secretly looking for the person or individuals responsible for her husband's incident. Jae began to conduct her investigation, and she learned that Christopher's car was shot up by a local gang. Her research later revealed that Edge had hired the gang. Edge was behind the attempted assassination of Christopher. Jae went to visit Edge in jail. She wanted him to know that she knew that he was the mastermind behind the attempted assassination of her husband.

Edge did not deny or admit to his involvement with Christopher's incident. Jae warns Edge to stay away from her husband and her family. Jae turns to exit when Edge gives her a message for Jewel. With a smirk on his face, he requests that Jae tell Jewel that he loves and misses her. Jae, who is unsure of how to interpret the message, thinks it is a very strange message. To the best of Jae's knowledge, he had never met her mother. Jae began to suspect that there was something more going on than she was aware of.

If she were able to find out that Edge was behind the attempted assassination of Christopher, why couldn't Rellik and Collin find out any information? She decided to visit Rellik and Collin to confront them with the information. Upon arriving at the NWO League headquarters, she immediately spots Jewel's car leaving the League's parking garage. Jae becomes genuinely concerned for her mother and her mother's safety. What reason would her mother possibly have for visiting the League? She wondered if her mother visiting the League had something to do with Edge's message. Rellik and Collin should have been able to find the very same information; they have far more resources than she has. She could understand Rellik's reason for not revealing Edge as the person of interest. Edge is Rellik's son, but what could possibly be Jewel's reason for being at the League? She wanted to know what was Jewel's connection to the League. What reason would Edge have for telling her mother that he loves and misses her?

Jae is under the assumption that they had, perhaps at one point in time, spent quality time together. Jae was beginning to suspect that something was going on of which she was not aware.

She had to find out what was Jewel's connection to Edge. She began to keep a watchful eye on Jewel because she knew that Jewel and Robert were having marital problems.

Jae began to wonder if Jewel was perhaps having an affair with Edge. She knew Edge did not have a good track record with women because he was always too busy to maintain a relationship. Jae was concerned that Jewel was much older than Edge. Meanwhile, Christopher is making progress and is placed in therapy to get the use of his legs back. Jae is determined to find out the connection between Edge and her mother. Jae begins probing into Jewel's past when she learns that she is not the only child Jewel had given birth too. Jewel was reported to have given birth to two sons prior to her that Jewel had never talked about when she was married to a man named Trell. After doing in-depth research, the gentleman went by the alias Rellik. Jae was shocked by what she read in the legal documents. It became apparent that Rellik was Jewel's ex-husband and Edge is their son. How could they have kept it a secret all those years?

Jae was upset and very confused and demanded answers from Jewel and Rellik. Jae considers whether this was the reason Rellik had been so generous to Christopher and her. Could Rellik also be her father, considering how much Edge and Jae resembled one another?

Even worst, how did Jewel meet Rellik in the line of work that they are in, and what was their attraction? Jae turns to Jewel and Rellik for answers. Afterwards, Jae goes back to see Edge, and she confronts him. Edge admits to his involvement with the attempted murder of Christopher. He maintains that he had no knowledge that she was his sister until after the deal had been made.

Being upset with her family, Jae ceased all communication with them for over a year. During this time, she gave birth to a handsome baby boy whom she named Christian. Christopher was able to talk Jae into giving her family yet another chance. Rellik, Jewel, and Robert were all proud grandparents. They all took turns babysitting baby Christian. Rellik and Jae continued to work on their relationship and getting to know each other. Two years later, Robert filed for a divorce from Jewel.

Robert and Jewel's relationship was never the same. He felt as if she were never truthful with him, and as a result, he felt as if he could not trust her. He questioned if she ever sincerely loved him. Edge vowed that when he got out of jail to get revenge on Rellik, Collin, and Christopher for setting him up.

The Kidnapping

Edge constantly fought to find ways to prove his innocence in the death of the Senator's daughter and her coworker. Two years later, Edge befriends a female security guard named Erica. Edge and Erica began dating and seeing one another secretly. Erica fell in love with him and vowed to do whatever it took to prove her love for him. She secretly began arranging things with the members of the mob, unaware that they were members of the mob. She thinks that they are only friends of Edge. The mob began working on getting him out of jail. A few members of the district attorney were also mobsters or owed the mob a favor. He began putting pressure on certain members of the district attorney to return the favor that is owed or suffer the consequences of their actions.

Edge had some unfinished business that he must take care of with Rellik, Collin, and Christopher for their roles in his incarceration. Edge vows to take down not only Rellik but the New World Order in its entirety for their roles in his demise. He plots to kill all three men but knows that he must be very discreet because he risks the chance of them finding out. If Rellik ever found out, the tables could easily be turned as in the past. He devises a plan to make them suffer for their actions. After being released from jail, Edge put his plan in motion. Edge knows that his plan must be successful this time around because his plan a few months earlier had failed. Edge steaks out Christopher's house as he plans to assassinate him when he sees his three-year-old nephew playing outside on his scooter. He notices that he is outside by himself.

Jae, his mother, had briefly entered her home to retrieve some items while leaving Christopher to play in the yard. Edge decides in a desperate attempt to get back at Christopher to kidnap his nephew. Although he does not want to hurt his sister, he wants to inflict the most agonizing pain known to man on his brother-in-law.

His nephew surprisingly goes with him without putting up a fight. A brief time later, Jae returns looking for him as she calls out, "Christian, where are you?" Jae walks around the yard looking for Christian when she notices that he is nowhere to be found. Jae then noticed the gate, which was closed, was now opened, and a black sports utility vehicle was speeding off. She immediately calls the police and Christopher for help. Days would pass with no sign of Christian in sight. Christopher, Rellik, and Jewel joined forces to look for him. All their leads came to a dead end. Jae felt helpless. How could she have been so careless leaving him outside, even for a moment? If she had only taken him in with her, Christian would have never gone missing.

After a year, there were still no leads on Christian's disappearance. Jae and Christopher's relationship began to suffer. They both blamed Jae's negligence for Christian's disappearance, and their relationship was now strained as Christopher began drinking and staying out all night.

Christopher spent more time in the office than he did at home.

The Hollermans were constantly finding ways to encourage Jae. Jae looked for ways to keep herself busy to keep her mind off Christian. She remained hopeful that he would be someday found alive and healthy.

The Plot

On the two-year anniversary of Christian's disappearance, Christopher is awakened by a series of clicking noises, followed by yelling and laughter. As he sits up in the bed, he notices Jae standing naked, looking in the mirror, holding her gun in her hand, and pointing it at her own head. Christopher began to yell as she pulled the trigger, the gun clicked, but it was empty, and she yelled angrily, followed by an outburst of laughter. Jae repeated the sequence. Christopher jumped out of bed, yelling as he grabbed the gun from her, "Jae, what are you doing?" Jae immediately dropped to her knees, sobbing as she explained that she could no longer go through life without knowing what had happened to her child. It became apparent that Jae needed mental help.

Jae was taken to the hospital and admitted for a mental evaluation. Jae was admitted to the hospital's psychiatric ward for three weeks before being released under the supervision of her husband to return to her residence. Jae kept herself busy to keep her mind off Christian. She found herself involved in several activities in the community and her church. Meanwhile, Edge is collaborating with members of the Cuban mafia who has assigned Christian to a Cuban family to oversee his needs. Christian passively remembers riding his scooter and his mother and father before the kidnapping. Christian was told that his parents died shortly after his birth in a tragic helicopter crash, and he had no surviving family.

The time had finally come for Christian to attend school. Christian, now old enough to attend school, was enrolled in school by his Cuban family. Edge often came around Christian to see how he was adjusting to his new family and community. Edge was introduced to Christian as a friend of the family. Edge began training Christian as a toddler to become an assassin. Christian's Cuban family treated him just like he was one of their very own.

His family celebrated his birthday yearly on his date of birth, just like the other children. He was taught about the Cuban culture, and beliefs. Christian was taught the daily necessities of life.

Twelve years later, Christian now a teenager began to adopt to the Cuban traditions, and beliefs. Christian was taught the daily necessities of life. He was taught how to prepare his meals, how to clean and was even taught how to drive. Christian took on many of the Cuban's practices. Meanwhile, Jae, and Christopher remained hopeful that they would someday be reunited with Christian. Jae felt as if he were still alive and often prayed to God for confirmation that he was still alive. She vowed that if she ever got a second chance, she would not only be an outstanding parent to him but never neglect him again. Jae knew if Christian were still alive, he would now be a teenager and would not remember them.

Chapter 7:

The Initiation

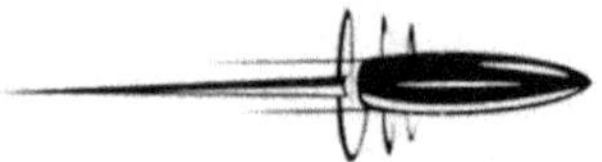

The Drug Bust

Christian was now a teenager, and he was forced to deal with the pressure of fitting in. Christian unknowingly was surrounded by mobsters and their families as he, too, began getting into trouble. Christian, as he was soon known as Kristoff, began smuggling drugs into the United States with other members of his Cuban family and others. Christian was not only a trained assassin, but he also was a drug lord. He rose to prominence in the industry as a result of his early training. Unknown to him, he was an assassin by blood. Kristoff and his Cuban family smuggled drugs and performed hits for many prominent figures.

Meanwhile, Rellik gets a call from one of his Cuban colleagues and is informed that Edge, who had been out of jail for quite some time now, is also believed to be working with the Cuban mafia. Rellik knows Edge all too well and knows how getting even with him Collin and Christopher would be a top priority on Edge's list, even if it killed him. Rellik began to make sense of it all. When he looks at the date of Edge's release and the date of Christian's kidnapping, he is immediately convinced that Edge is the mastermind behind his very own nephew's kidnapping.

Rellik informs Christopher and Jewel of his beliefs but is reluctant to tell Jae. He fears that Jae will confront Edge blowing the case causing him to move Christian or, even worst, kill him if he had not already done so. If Edge could kill his very own brother, he could most definitely kill his nephew. Most assassins are trained killers who do not have a conscience and will stop anyone who gets in their way. Rellik calls a meeting with Jewel and Christopher, where he shares the information that was given to him.

He informs them that it is his very own belief that Edge has a role in Christian's kidnapping.

If he thinks that they are on to him and coming for Christian, he will stop at nothing to get what he wants, even if it means killing Christian, so they must act quickly.

They hear a loud thump, and as they turn to investigate the noise, Jae is spotted lying on the floor. She had been listening around the corner before passing out. Jae is unable to deal with the pressure of not knowing if her child is dead or alive. They make every attempt to reach out to Edge, but he is nowhere to be found. His previous residence now sat vacant as they had no known address for him. Rellik immediately began putting a plan in place to get Christian back. Meanwhile, Christian, "Kristoff" was hired to smuggle drugs from Cuba to New York City, but things would be different this time because he was working with amateurs. He had never been to New York City and had no idea what to expect. Kristoff arrives in New York City to set up a meeting with the buyer, which turns into an undercover drug bust. Kristoff flees from the scene as he shoots and kills two undercover New York Police Department officers. Kristoff attempts to flee New York City but is forced to seek refuge until all search efforts are exhausted.

Kristoff walks into an abandoned building after hearing footsteps. As he turns to investigate, he notices an older, gray-haired gentleman dressed casually standing nearby. Kristoff immediately draws his gun on the gentleman. The man did not appear to be homeless because he was well-groomed. Kristoff yells to the man, "Don't move, or else you'll be a dead man." The man tells Kristoff that he is thirteen years too late. Kristoff looks on in confusion and asks, "What are you talking about? Never mind, old man, I do not have time to find out what you are talking about. Just tell me how I can get out of this building and to safety if you want to live." He tells Kristoff he must trust him, and he will be fine. He tells Kristoff to follow him, and he will lead him to safety.

The man takes Kristoff to an underground basement in the abandoned building that leads several blocks down behind an abandoned garage, where he phoned to have someone pick them up. Kristoff was unsure of the motive as to why the man was helping him. Kristoff asks the man, "What do you want? Do you want to purchase something, or do you need a favor?"

The man said, "Well, to answer your question, if I am to start from the beginning, I must first explain the statement I made when we were in the abandoned building. Christian, my son...." But Kristoff refuted, "My name is Kristoff, not Christian" The man did not make any comment but continued, "I have been following you for the last two months. With careful planning, my goal was to lure you to New York City so that you could be back with your family. It was never my intention for anyone to get killed. I see you have my bloodline; indeed, you are an assassin." Kristoff responds,

"Who are you, and what are you talking about, old man?" "I am your grandfather, and my name is Rellik. You were kidnapped at the age of three years old from your mother as she ran into the house briefly to tend to some business. You were kidnapped by your very own uncle, my son. He was angry with your father and me for being sent to prison." Rellik explained to Kristoff, "When you, my first grandchild, was kidnaped, it was as if a part of me died that very same day. However, I had to be optimistic for your parents as well as myself.

After careful research, I learned that you were in Cuba, so I had to strategically plan a way to lure you back to the United States. It would have been too risky for me to travel to Cuba to get you."

Kristoff responds, "This is a lie. I do not know what you stand to gain by your lies, but I demand that you stop with your lies at once. I am not sure who you are confusing me with, but my name is Kristoff, and my parents were killed shortly after my birth in a tragic airplane accident." Rellik replied, "Kristoff, which is not true; that is a story that was made up to hide your true identity by your kidnappers.

If you would please give me a chance to prove to you that I am telling you the truth, I would like to take you to meet your parents, and we could do a DNA test with your consent. I will make you a deal. If you agree to take a DNA test and it proves that you are not my grandson. I will personally oversee that you are flown back to Cuba in my private jet back to your family. However, if you take the DNA test and it is true that you are my grandson Christian, I will take care of you and ensure that you have the best attorneys to beat the charges at hand and reunite you with your parents.

Either way, my son, you will have nothing to lose but everything to gain from our meeting. If you refuse to take the DNA test, I will get my driver to drive you wherever you want to go, never to bother you again." Kristoff refused to take the test and agreed to have Rellik's driver take him to safety. As Kristoff sits, waiting for Rellik's driver to arrive. Christopher walks in to speak to Rellik to get the status of Christian's whereabouts. As Christopher sees Kristoff, it is like looking into the mirror. Christopher and Kristoff were both speechless. Kristoff reconsidered and agreed to take the DNA test. Rellik and Christopher took him to meet Jae. The DNA test proved that Jae and Christopher were his parents. Jae vowed never to let him out of her sight ever again, stating that God had answered her prayers in abundance. However, their problems were far from being over. Kristoff's Cuban family looked for him because they wanted answers as to his whereabouts and what happened to the money and drugs he was given for distribution. NYPD was also close to identifying Kristoff as the killer of the two police officers. If he were identified with the killings of the two officers, he would be facing two life sentences with no chance of parole.

Meanwhile, Kristoff's Cuban family reaches out to Edge to inform him of Kristoff's disappearance. Edge immediately conducts an investigation of his very own. Kristoff's family wonders if he has taken off with their money, guns, and drugs. They demand to either have him brought back to Cuba to get answers or demand payment in full for their missing contraband. Edge searches for Kristoff to get answers. Edge is unable to locate Kristoff as his trail goes cold. The Cuban mobsters now began to threaten Edge's life. Edge knows that Rellik is the only person other than himself that has a great business relationship with the Cubans. The Cubans had a profound respect for Rellik because he had worked with them on numerous occasions.

However, Edge himself did not have a relationship with Rellik, and he despised him. Edge knew he had to act quickly because time was of the essence, and the Cubans meant business. Edge reached out to other new and former assassins for their help. The word got back to Rellik, confirming Edge's involvement with the Cuban mafia. Rellik, after speaking with Kristoff, contacted the Cuban mafia and oversaw that they got all their contraband that was in Kristoff's possession returned.

Kristoff's Loyalty

Kristoff began to build a bond with his parents and Rellik; he was happy that Rellik reached out to him. He vowed to kill Edge if he ever encountered him. As the NYPD was getting closer to solving the case, they had video surveillance of Kristoff, and they were still working to positively identify him. When Rellik and Christopher learned about the surveillance video, Rellik contacted a few friends who worked in the police department for whom he had performed hits. As a result, the surveillance videos and all evidence identifying Kristoff as the killer went missing, and the case grew cold. Rellik got a lead that Edge had planned to attend a conference for the League. Rellik, Jewel, Christopher, and Kristoff decided to give Edge a surprise visit. They went to confront him about Kristoff's kidnapping. Upon spotting the trio, Edge looked as if he had seen a ghost. Kristoff immediately punches Edge in the mouth before he is given the opportunity to say anything. Edge sarcastically responds, "I guess I may have deserved that," as he smirks and wipes the blood from his mouth.

Christopher intervenes and says, "Good job, son." Jewel questions Edge as to how he could have stooped so low to kidnap his own nephew and fill his head with such awful lies? Christopher asks Jewel what else could she expect from someone who murdered his very own brother? Edge gets angrily defensive about Christopher's remark. Christopher tells Edge that he would not have a fighting chance stating that he would kill Edge in a split second with his bare hands. Christopher demands to know why Edge kidnapped his son. Edge tells Christopher that kidnapping Kristoff was the best thing that had ever happened to Kristoff. Edge tells Christopher that Kristoff now knows how to be a man because of him. Christopher tackles Edge, knocking him to the floor. Rellik and Kristoff struggle to separate the two men. Edge stumbles to his feet as he grasps for breath. Edge tells Christopher that kidnapping Kristoff was never his intention. Edge states that he was angry and wanted to get back at his family. He wanted them to feel pain just as he had endured pain being locked away in a cell for a crime he did not commit. Christopher reminds Edge that it was his idea after all, so why was he now so upset because it did not go the way he had planned?

Edge storms off, letting Christopher know that it is not over; in fact, the war has just begun.

The Ambush

Jae was grateful to have Kristoff back in their lives. She spent as much time as humanly possible with him. Kristoff did not have very many friends. Jae often took Kristoff to church with her. Kristoff was introduced to Senator Hollerman's grandchildren, who were around his age. Kristoff became best friends with the deceased Nalerie Hollerman's son. Nalerie Hollerman's ex-husband had full custody of her son Noah prior to her passing. Noah and his father had recently moved back to the area. Noah was now able to spend more time with his grandparents after moving back to the area. Noah's grandparents needed him, and he, likewise, needed them as well for emotional support. They all were still coping with Nalerie's death in their very own way. Noah knew that his mother was killed, but he never knew the full details surrounding her death, nor did he know of the relationship she had with Edge.

One day, while hanging out, Noah and Kristoff began sharing their life stories. Kristoff explains to Noah that he, too, like Noah was without his parents for a substantial portion of his life due to his kidnapping. Unlike Kristoff, Noah grew up with his parents, including his mother, but he no longer has her due to her untimely death. Kristoff asks Noah how he could be so forgiving and understanding, knowing that Edge played a role in his mother's murder.

Noah looks on in surprise, unaware that Edge even knew his mother, not to mention that he could have possibly played a role in her murder. Noah began to ask Kristoff questions about his mother's death and inquired how he knew. Kristoff tells Noah that he heard rumors about Edge's possible involvement in Noah's mother's death. When Noah learns of Edge's possible involvement in his mother's murder, he desperately wants to get even with Edge. Unlike Kristoff, he had no prior experience. Noah knew nothing about committing a murder other than what he saw on television. Kristoff, on the other hand, was born into a family of assassins. They both agreed to produce a plan to have Edge killed.

Kristoff asked Noah if he was sure if he wanted to participate in the assassination plot? He knew that Noah had no experience. Noah insisted that he must revenge his mother's death. Kristoff told Noah not to worry and that he would handle all of the arrangements, and once they were complete and ready to be carried out, he would share them with him. Kristoff told Noah not to utter a word to anyone for fear of any information getting leaked. The following day, they met at Noah's house. Noah stated that he had some information to share with Kristoff. When they met, Noah informed Kristoff that he had hired backup just in case he and Kristoff needed some additional help. Kristoff, angry with Noah, reminded him that he had been sworn to secrecy. Noah tells Kristoff that the guy hired came highly recommended by a mutual friend. Kristoff explains to Noah that when planning an assassination, you must not trust anyone. Noah tells Kristoff that the best thing about it is that they do not have to pay any money for the hit. Kristoff knows Noah is not street-smart, but he cannot believe what he hears. Kristoff knows that it is a setup of some sort and tells Noah that he would not be a part of it and demands that Noah follow suit.

Noah asked Kristoff to hear him out, stating that the guy was very understanding. The guy requests them to attend a meeting at his house and become members of his club in an effort to protect and stop community violence. Kristoff asks Noah if he has given Edge's name and known information to the hitman. Noah sarcastically responds, "No," but as Kristoff is beginning to feel better, he adds, "Of course, I did; how was he supposed to know who he is to assassinate?" Kristoff drops his head, "are you kidding me?" Kristoff asks Noah, "More importantly, did you give him our information?" Noah responds, "Only our names and my address." Kristoff again cannot believe what he is hearing. Kristoff feels that he might as well announce their plan to kill Edge over the local radio station's airways rather than entrust Noah to secrecy. Kristoff worried that the police would be busting into Noah's house at any time to arrest them for the plot to kill Edge. Kristoff, against his better judgment, decided to attend the meeting with Noah. When they arrived at the address given to Noah, their MapQuest brought them to an apartment in the projects of New York City. Noah double-checked the address provided to ensure that they had arrived at the correct address.

Noah noticed that neither the apartment number nor the street name was visible. Before they could leave, a gang surrounded the car and demanded that they get out. Just as Kristoff expected, he knew that it was too good to be true. Noah, still unaware of what was happening, asked the gang where the man he had spoken with, known as "Big Homie."

Before now, Kristoff did not know the name of the man that Noah had spoken with via google voice and chat. When Kristoff heard the title, he knew it was a high-ranking gangster. The gang began to laugh as they knew that Noah was clueless about what would take place. Noah responded, "Yes, I might add it is a very humorous name. However, he invited my friend and I to a meeting to join his club.

I understand that his club protects the community in exchange for a favor. What a nice guy." Shortly afterward, another car pulled up, distracting the gangsters; much to their dismay, it was none other than Edge. Edge pulls in as he is unknowingly lured to the apartment by the gangsters in the assassination plot. He is surprised to see the boys. Likewise, they are also surprised but oddly happy to see him.

Edge gives Kristoff a distinct nod, just as he did when he was training him to be an assassin. It was a way for them to communicate secretly. It informed the other person when someone was in trouble and signaled for help. Kristoff reluctantly nodded back, signaling that he was going to need help. Edge signaled for his men to open fire, allowing both boys to leave the scene in their car. Edge led the way out of the area. After arriving to safety, Edge warned the boys to be more cautious of the part of town that they visited and the people they entertained. The boys began to feel guilty for their roles in the plot to end his life. Edge appeared to have a heart underneath the hate that he carried. Edge questioned the boys as to what kind of business they were overseeing in that part of town. Noah looks at Kristoff as he stares away in silence. Noah confessed to Edge that he had hired a hitman to assassinate him. Edge surprisingly asks no questions. He tells the boys that he knows that he has been any and everything except a good example to them, and he apologizes for allowing his emotions to get the best of him. Although Edge had not always made the best or most responsible decisions, he still cared about their well-being.

Noah demands to know the role that Edge played in the demise of his mother. Edge contends that he had nothing to do with killing Noah's mother. He tells Noah that he had a profound respect for his mother and offered to assist Noah with finding his mother's killer(s). Edge agreed he would never utter a word of the boy's assassination plot to kill him. He warned the boys that if they ever decided to order another hit on him and failed, they would be the ones pushing up daisies if he ever found out. Kristoff sarcastically tells Edge that he cannot make any promises.

Kristoff reminds Edge that it was because of his decision to abduct him that he did not have his parents in his life as a child. Edge turns back to Kristoff and says, "I am glad you reminded me." You must never bring up the subject of my kidnapping you ever. If you should forget, I will be sure to give the NYPD the information they will need to positively identify and arrest the killer of the slain officers." Kristoff was stunned because he did not know that Edge knew of his involvement in the killings of the slain officers. "I thought that would get your attention. Nephew, why is it that you make me play dirty every time?" Edge gets into his car and drives away.

Noah's Contract

Just as the boys thought that their problems were over, they were just beginning. The gangsters were actively looking for Edge to carry out the assassination plot. Noah, still very naïve, contacted the "Big Homie," thanking him for his time and letting him know that their services were no longer needed. He assumed that everything would be fine, but there was just one problem. There was a contract that was signed for the assassination of Edge. The contract was binding and could only be broken at the discretion of the leader. If the contract were terminated for some reason, it would be in favor of the opposing party that upheld their end of the contract. The contract stated that the assassination would be free of charge provided the individuals ordering the hit became an active member of the organization committing the crime after the crime was committed. When joining the organization, the individual must do whatever is required to demonstrate his or her loyalty. Fearful and unsure of what to do, Noah began to fear for his own life and his family's safety.

He was constantly terrified and even feared leaving his house or looking out the window. Although the gang's contract was with Noah, Kristoff was Noah's friend and felt that it was his fault that Noah was pulled into such conflict. The boys were left with no option other than to reach out to Edge to inform him that his life may be in immediate danger.

Edge, as usual, could not be reached because he often changed his cell phone number and home address to cover his trail. Noah was left with no option but to join the gang. Kristoff joined along with Noah because he felt he was just as much at fault as Noah. Kristoff knew that he had what it took to thrive in the gang but feared for Noah. It was clear that Noah was out of his element. The boy's first assignment was to rob someone. The gang drove them around the neighborhood and gave them random people to rob. They were told to wait in the van until told to exit, as they would jump out of the van, drawing their gun on their victims while taking their belongings. They wanted to see if the boys had the skills to join the gang. Kristoff's crime went off as planned, and he returned to the van with money and jewelry from his victim.

Then it was Noah's turn. Noah exits the van and walks over to an elderly couple, yelling this is a robbery, give me all your money. He fails to insert the clip properly, and the magazine drops out of the gun and hits the pavement, where bullets are left rolling around on the ground.

They both were hard of hearing and wore hearing aids. They both contemplate what they think he has said. The lady thinks he has said his name is Rob, and he needs some money. Noah bends over to retrieve the bullets from the ground when he looks up. The elderly lady, with a smile on her face, stood with her hand extended to him, shakes his hand, and says, "Well, it is nice to meet you, Rob; you are in luck, Sonny, because I do have some money today. Would twenty be enough as she pulls out a twenty-dollar bill from her purse?" He feels guilty and says, "No," "No," this is wrong," as he talks to himself aloud. She thinks he is saying that the twenty dollars is not enough, so she reaches back into her purse and exchanges the twenty-dollar bill for a fifty-dollar bill to give to him. He refuses the money as he hands her back the fifty-dollar bill.

He is unaware they are watching him but knows he must get something. He grabs a one-dollar bill from her purse, thanks her, and leaves, running back to the van. The members of the gang sat in the van as they looked on, shaking their heads. Noah gets back into the van and says,

"There, I have done it now. I robbed my first victim and upheld my contract. Am I now free to leave?" The gang decided to give Noah another task to test him. Kristoff undoubtedly had proven himself to have what it takes to be a member of the gang. Noah has yet to prove he can hold his weight in the gang. Noah is given a second chance to prove himself. Noah is given another task to complete. He is taken to a homeless shelter to steal the supplies donated to the shelter. He is supposed to gain entry to the shelter through a broken window. Noah decides to walk through the front door of the shelter. The gang waits outside in the van for Noah's return. As the gang sits in the van anticipating his return, two hours would go by before they decide to go into the homeless shelter to check on him. They were surprised by what they saw. Noah was sitting at the table playing a UNO card game with a group of people.

The gangsters looked on as Noah sat positively, encouraging the group. Noah did not notice that they had entered the building until one of the men offered a chair to one of the gangsters. Noah looked up at them as he proceeded to play the game of cards and introduced the gangsters to the group. Before being pulled aside by one of the gangsters, one of the ladies responded, "Hey, what are you doing to Noah? He is our friend; he not only gave my son the jacket off his back and wrote us a check for $200.00 for our supplies." The elderly lady is quickly reminded by her son, "Oh, I forgot I wasn't supposed to tell anyone."

Noah drops his head before gazing up into the eyes of the terribly angry "Underboss" of the gang. "The Underboss" says, "If anything is to be done correctly, you must do it yourself." He heads for the storage closet when an elderly man attempts to stop him, he shoves the man, knocking him to the floor. The elderly man clutches his chest as he passes out on the floor. An elderly lady gets up and runs over to the man, yelling at the gangster, "What have you done to my husband?" Noah rushes over to check on him. Noah notices that he is not breathing, and his heart is not beating.

Noah yells for someone to call for help as he begins to perform cardiopulmonary resuscitation (CPR) until emergency crews arrive. The elderly man is rushed to the hospital. Noah's quick response is credited with saving the man's life. The man and his wife were grateful to Noah. Noah's story was the highlight of the evening news. Upon the airing of Noah's story, people began to recognize him for his heroism around town. The gang did not want Noah to draw unwanted attention to them because they were already wanted by members of the opposing gang as well as the police. They were given no other option but to release Noah from his contract.

It was obvious to them that Noah did not fit in and lacked what it took to be a gangster. Noah had a heart made of gold and would literally give someone the shirt off his back, which was not good for his role in the gang. The agreement was originally between Noah and the gangs. Now, the gang has decided to terminate Noah's contract and allow him to leave the gang. On the other hand, Kristoff willingly entered his contract to be with Noah. Kristoff was expected to fulfill his contract because he had proved himself to be competent.

Kristoff could now concentrate on himself because he no longer had to worry about Noah. It was up to him to decide whether he wanted to stay with the gang or leave. They began assigning Kristoff assignments to complete. It would not be long before they realized that Kristoff was not like anyone else, they had ever recruited. They came to realize that this was not Kristoff's "first rodeo;" he was a natural. Kristoff feared nothing because he had been through a lot and, in many instances, made them question their very own safety. The "Big Homie" looked to Kristoff for direction. "The Underboss," who was second in command to the "Big Homie," began to feel threatened by Kristoff's ability to provide leadership.

"The Underboss" decided that he wanted Kristoff out of the way, whether it was voluntary or involuntary(death).

"The Underboss" had a meeting with Kristoff, informing him that he was going to honor Kristoff's request to leave the gang because he had satisfied the terms of his contract. Kristoff quickly corrects him, informing "The Underboss" that he never requested to leave.

"The Underboss" tells him that since he had joined to help Noah and Noah's contract was no longer valid, he assumed that Kristoff also wanted to leave. Kristoff assures him that he is not interested in leaving the gang. He states that not only had he made new friends, many of whom share his interests, but he had also learned a lot. The "Big Homie" agrees with Kristoff and honors his wishes. Kristoff stays in the gang.

Edge's Surprise

The "Underboss" secretly plots to have Kristoff killed. He fears that Kristoff is taking his position. He unknowingly seeks the help of a hitman who happens to be a close friend of Christopher. After investigating and confirming that he is to assassinate Kristoff, Christopher's son, he informs Christopher of the hit. When Christopher learns of the job for hire, he informs Kristoff of the plot to kill him. Edge gets word of the assassination plot to kill Kristoff and decides to give him a taste of his own medicine. Edge decides to assassinate "The Underboss" and set Kristoff up.

Edge executes "The Underboss" and then leaks the record showing that "The Underboss" was plotting to kill Kristoff, giving Kristoff a motive for killing "The Underboss." Everyone begins to blame Kristoff for "The Underboss's" death, just as Edge had planned. The "Big Homie" and others in the gang become doubtful of Kristoff's loyalty. They now contemplate killing Kristoff. Kristoff tries to prove his loyalty but struggles as he tries to prove his innocence. He has no idea that Edge is the real killer and has set him up. Kristoff fears that he will not only blow his very own cover but runs the risk of revealing his and his family's involvement with the mafia. He knew that his family could save him from many things, but being saved from the mafia would be a challenge. Members of the gang are torn as many of them believe that Kristoff is not a loyal member, while others feel he is a perfect example of loyalty. Blaze, one of the members of Kristoff's gang, decides to revenge "The Underboss" death. Blaze believes that by killing Kristoff, he will avenge the death of "The Underboss" and prove that he is worthy of fulfilling the position of "The Underboss." Kristoff and Noah are traveling eastbound in Noah's car when they spot a young girl's car that has broken down on the side of the road.

She is noticeably standing beside a car with a flat tire holding a toddler's hand. Noah has a heart made of gold and sees everyone as harmless despite his past run-in with the gangs. Noah, without any hesitation, decided to stop to help her. Kristoff, being street-smart informed Noah that he did not feel that it was a good idea. Noah refused to listen to Kristoff. Kristoff told Noah that if they must stop, it would be wise to fix the tire or stay with her and the toddler until they got a ride. It would be in their best interest not to offer her a ride. After getting out of the car and speaking with the young girl, she explained that her tire had blown out on her way to take her nephew home. She stated to Noah that she really needed to get there and would be grateful for a ride. Kristoff asked her how long she and the toddler had been stranded? She told Kristoff that she had been stranded for 45 minutes, and no one had stopped to offer her any help until now. Kristoff asked her if she had called anyone for help? She told him that she had no one to call for help. Noah intervenes, reassuring her not to worry. He says, "My beautiful butterfly, we will be happy to give you a ride to your sister's house."

Kristoff pulls Noah aside. Noah, we cannot give her a ride. Remember, we agreed in the car to either fix the tire or stay with her until she got help. It could be a set-up because she had been out here for 45 minutes, and no one had stopped to help her. There may be a reason no one has stopped to assist her. Noah, sarcastically with a smirk on his face, tells Kristoff, "My friend, that is because they are not gentlemen like we are. Kristoff, my friend, not only do we get the chance to be her knight in shining armor but get a chance to win her heart. It will not be hard for her to accept my request to go out on a date after it is all over. Kristoff, my friend, do not worry; I got this."

Noah returned to the young girl as he had agreed to give her a ride to her sister's house. Kristoff insisted that she rode in the front seat beside Noah as he and the toddler rode in the back of the vehicle. The young girl is giving Noah directions to her sister's home. Kristoff noticed that many of the roads were either one-way streets or dead-end roads. Kristoff insisted that Noah should not go any further but instead drop her off at the closest market. Noah, being a good Samaritan, insisted on taking her all the way.

Soon, they were lured to a neighborhood in the neighboring town where, just as Kristoff had suspected, they had been set up. In the neighboring town, members of not only the rival gang were waiting on them but even some of Kristoff's very own gang members. The guys find out upon her exiting the vehicle that the female is the girlfriend of "The Big Homie" of the rival gang. She quickly pointed out to Noah as she exited the vehicle that although he was a nice guy, she would never have gone out with him. Kristoff had no backup plan because he was unprepared for what was about to happen. Kristoff thought to himself, "What a bad time to be in trouble." He only had four bullets in his gun, and to make matters worse, he had no help. Like everyone else, he knew Noah was not a gangster. Noah knew nothing about guns, nor did he have the desire to learn anything about them. Kristoff notices that several of the gang members are surrounding them with guns and weapons of all sorts. The gangsters told Noah he was free to go because it was Kristoff they wanted because of his role in the slaying of "The Underboss." Noah tells them that he and Kristoff are a team, and he will not leave his friend.

Kristoff appreciates Noah's loyalty but knows there is nothing that Noah can do, and he insists that Noah should leave. Noah leaves as he is unsure of what to do or where he should go for help. Noah is surprised when he runs into Edge half a block away. He informs Edge of what has happened, and Edge tells him not to worry and that Kristoff can take care of himself and will be fine. He pleads with Edge to go with him to provide help for Kristoff, stating that it was his fault that Kristoff's life was in danger. Edge reluctantly agrees to go with Noah. When they arrive at the scene, they find themselves in the middle of a shoot-out as bullets are flying in all directions. Edge instructs Noah to stay in the car. Edge spots Blaze as he is just about to shoot Kristoff, who appears to be out of bullets. Edge aims at Blaze, but just as he is about to pull the trigger, he hears someone yell, "EDGE!! Please, do not shoot; he is your son."

Blaze, Kristoff, and Edge are all stunned as they lower their guns. The trio all turn around to investigate the woman's claims. Edge is stunned when he learns that it is Erica. Edge is speechless as he inquires why Erica did not tell him sooner about Blaze.

Edge had not seen or spoken to Erica since she helped him get out of jail. "Did you say that he is my son?" Edge asked. "Yes, he is your son," she replies. It had been fifteen years since they had last seen each other. Edge began calculating the dates and knew that it had been fifteen years since he and Erica were in a relationship, and they were exclusive. Blaze resembled Edge in many ways. Edge's family had strong genes and dominant features. Many of the males had what is medically categorized as a complete heterochromia regarding their eye color (one was hazel and the other green) and prominent bone structures as far as their facial features. Erica stated that she had tried numerous times to reach out to Edge but was never able to contact him. Erica felt that Edge had only used her to get out of jail and felt that he deliberately avoided her. Kristoff was unsure of what was unfolding in front of his eyes. As Kristoff overhears Erica's comments about Edge, he promptly agrees with her. He knows that Edge can not only be a manipulator to get what he wants but is also a habitual liar. Kristoff feels that Edge has gotten the karma that he deserves. Edge had kept him away from his parents through the earlier years of his life.

Edge, too, had now missed the earlier years of his very own son's life as well. Kristoff is saddened for Blaze because he knows first-hand what it feels like growing up without your biological parents. However, Blaze did have one of his parents. Kristoff's day had turned out to be a not-so-bad day after all. Kristoff looks on at Blaze as he is both hurt and confused.

Kristoff tells Blaze, "I know we may not be fond of one another, but I do understand how you must feel." Kristoff turns and walks away. Edge, overwhelmed by everything that had taken place, decided upon gathering his thoughts that he wanted to work on getting to know Blaze. Edge desperately searched for ways to establish a relationship with Blaze. He wanted more than anything to be a part of his son's life. Edge knew that he could not erase the past, but he wanted to do everything he could to be a part of Blaze's future. Edge's life changed drastically, although he had never considered himself a father figure. He knew if given the opportunity, he would be a great father. Edge arranged several activities to be able to spend time with Blaze to get to know him better.

Blaze would never show up, always standing Edge up, resulting in him going alone. When asked about him not showing up, he told Edge that he was no longer a kid; he now had his own life, which did not include Edge. He blames Erica and Edge for Edge not being in his life as a toddler. Blaze maintains that he has been doing fine and will continue to do so without Edge. He tells Edge that he cannot miss what he has never had. Edge began sending Blaze gifts to make up for the lost time. Blaze thinks Erica's buying him the items, but after learning that the gifts are from Edge, he decides to give him a chance and get to know him. He began spending time with Edge as they began building a relationship. As they come to know one another, Edge comes to learn that he and Blaze have a lot in common. They both share many of the same likes and dislikes; they even share the very same allergies. Edge would soon come to learn they are both also short-tempered. It is without question that Blaze is indeed Edge's son. Edge wonders if Blaze inherited any of his family's characteristics other than his looks. Edge is unsure of how or when he will reveal the family's secret to Blaze.

He still feels that it is too early to speak with Blaze about the family's secret until he knows that he will not share it with anyone else, not even his very own mother.

Kristoff and Blaze are still not on the absolute best of terms. Kristoff and Blaze have agreed to try to get along for the sake of being blood relatives. However, Kristoff feels Blaze is his father's son and just as evil as his father. When asked about Blaze, Kristoff says that the apple does not fall too far from the tree.

Blaze still blames Kristoff for the death of "The Underboss" and continuously looks for ways to destroy him. Several months would pass as Blaze and Edge's relationship continued to blossom. Blaze now stayed at his father's house at least four days out of the week. It would not be long before things could all change. Blaze, while snooping through the cabinets in Edge's library, finds an envelope that could forever change the way he views Edge. He is surprised by the contents of the vanilla envelope that he finds in his father's library. He quickly learns of Edge's involvement with the mafia.

He finds pictures taken of the lifeless body of "The Underboss" and a contract attached to the pictures describing how the murder should be set up to make it look like Kristoff had committed the murder. In the letter attached to the contract, Edge stated that he wanted to teach Kristoff a lesson to make sure that he never crossed him again. Edge walks into the library, where he catches Blaze looking at the files. Edge says to Blaze, "Here you are. I have been looking all over for you. Are you okay?" Blaze is visibly shaken by what he sees and is unsure of how to address Edge. Unable to contain himself, Blaze asks Edge, "Why did you kill "The Underboss"?

What did he do to you? What kind of monster are you that you make a living killing and torturing people? I do not want to have anything ever to do with you." Edge walks over to Blaze. Blaze asks Edge, "Are you going to kill me too, your very own son?" For the first time in Edge's life, he is remorseful and sad when he sees Blaze's reaction. Blaze brought out a side of Edge that no one knew existed, not even Edge himself. It was all new to Edge to finally love someone more than he loved himself.

Edge pleaded with Blaze not to leave and to give him a chance to explain himself. Edge made Blaze and himself some warm cocoa and popcorn as they sat by the fire in their pajamas. Edge started from the very beginning about how his parents met and the events that took place upon their meeting. Edge shared his life story up until he met Erica and was released from prison. He gave Blaze a thorough understanding of who he was and how he got to that point. Edge thanked Blaze for coming into his life and changing his life for the better. Edge shared with Blaze how he had always taken life for granted. He felt as if he had nothing to live for until Blaze came into his life and gave him a reason to live. Edge tells him that it is important to him that Blaze be a part of his life. The following morning Edge took Blaze to meet Jewel, his grandmother. Edge still was not on good terms with Rellik, his father. Edge was excited and felt proud to surprise Jewel with her new grandson.

After arriving at Jewel's home, Edge told Jewel that he had a wonderful surprise for her. Jewel also informed him that she also had a surprise for him as well.

Edge began to share with Jewel the events leading up to his meeting with Blaze. Afterward, he presented Blaze Jewel's new grandson to her, and she was overjoyed to meet him. Jewel could not wait to introduce him to the rest of the family. Jewel then presented her surprise to Edge. Jewel introduced her new husband to Edge, as he never knew that she was dating anyone. He often wondered why she seemed to mysteriously disappear at times for days or even weeks.

In walks Rellik, wearing a matching pajama set as Jewel. Edge is both astounded and upset by what he sees. "Mother, you said you wanted to introduce your new husband to me; what is the meaning of all this? What is he doing here, and where is your new husband?" Edge questions. "My dear, you are looking at him. My new husband is none other than your very own father, the one and only Rellik El'Poep," replied Jewel. Edge questions Jewel about how long she and Rellik had been married. Jewel explains to Edge that she and Rellik had decided a month ago to remarry and decided to wait for the right time to tell the family. She quickly intervenes, "It has been the absolute best month of my entire life."

Edge is speechless as he has not spoken in quite some time to his father. Edge tells Jewel that if she is happy, he, too, is happy for her. Rellik asks Edge sarcastically, "Are you, my son, really happy? No, of course, you are not. However, your mother and I are extremely happy, and we will not let you or anyone interfere with our happiness." After meeting Blaze, he and Rellik hit it off instantly as if they had known one another all along. They decided to have a family gathering to introduce Blaze to the rest of the family, where Jewel and Rellik would announce their love for one another. They would share with their family that they are not only a couple again but have decided to renew their marriage vows. Blaze made amends with Kristoff, and they began to form a bond. In the meantime, Noah is accepted and will be attending one of the most prestigious universities in New York City. He plans to pursue a career in criminal justice. His goal is to become a district attorney, just like his mother. They planned to celebrate with their girlfriends by going out on a double date. They planned a night out in the town, which consisted of dinner and a movie. Kristoff realizes that he has left his wallet at his house.

Noah's Celebration

Kristoff returns to his home, where he grabs his wallet and heads out the door. He then realizes that he has not spoken with Jae. He wanted her to know that he would be coming in later than his normal time. Since his kidnapping, Jae wanted to know where he was always. She automatically worries that something has happened whenever he is out later than his normal time, just like most parents. He heads back into his house. Noah follows him into the house when they overhear Christopher talking on the phone. He is ironically speaking about the assassination of Nalerie Hollerman, Noah's mother. He tells the person on the other end of the phone that Noah is nothing like his mother and will be a better district attorney.

He tells the person on the other end of the phone that he feels bad for killing her, seeing how much Noah loves and misses her. He states that it was in the best interest of the League. He tells how she had threatened to send them all to prison. Kristoff and Noah were in awe by what they heard. Noah was in disbelief, and it was apparent that he was in pain.

Noah was speechless as he stood with his jaw dropped and his mouth opened as tears began to flow down his face. Noah turned and ran out the door, jumped into his car, as he sped out of Kristoff's driveway. Kristoff walks into the library, where he confronts Christopher as he stands with his back turned to the door, talking on the phone. Kristoff walks in, slamming the door to get Christopher's attention.

Christopher turns around and looks at Kristoff as he responds, "Son, you startled me; I did not see you standing there." Christopher sees how upset Kristoff is as he requests to call the person on the other end of the phone back. Kristoff asks Christopher how he could smile in Noah's face, knowing that he was the one that killed his mother, as he sits and watches Noah knowing that he grieves for his mother daily. Christopher explained to Kristoff that the incident had occurred before he ever met Noah. Christopher tries to explain to Kristoff, but he refuses to hear him as he leaves in search of Noah. Kristoff goes to Noah's house and knocks at the door but does not get an answer. He tried calling Noah several times, but his phone calls went unanswered.

The phone calls were forwarded to his voicemail which was now full. Kristoff was devastated by what he learned versus what he had been told. Kristoff had unknowingly falsely accused Edge of Noah's mother's murder. Noah would have killed him for no reason, only to discover that it was his very own father. He was beginning to wonder if his father was any better than Edge. The day was supposed to be a celebration of Noah's accomplishments, but it instead turned out to be anything except a celebration. Months would go by before Kristoff would see or hear from Noah again. Kristoff saw Noah at church, but as he attempted to conversate with him, Noah refused. Noah walked past him, pretending not to see him. Kristoff stopped Noah, asking if he would please allow him some time to speak with him. Noah agreed to meet with Kristoff after church at the local eatery to speak with him. Kristoff brought Christopher with him. Noah spotted Christopher, and he immediately got up to leave. Upon talking Noah into staying, they all sat and talked for hours.

Christopher explained to Noah the details surrounding the death of his mother.

Noah was upset in the beginning, but in the end, he was able to come to grips with his mother's death. Christopher had confirmed some things that Noah had heard prior to their meeting. He stated that although hearing the details surrounding his mother's death was not easy, he now felt better knowing exactly what happened. Kristoff and Noah parted ways as they tried to remain friends. However, they were not as close as they once were, but Noah blamed his schooling, claiming that he was much too busy adjusting to college life as the reason he and Kristoff were not as close as they once were. Kristoff knew that Noah was still grieving his mother's death. Kristoff understood that Noah had a heart of gold and did not deserve to be hurt the way in which he was hurt. All he has ever wanted to do was to help. Noah was Kristof's best friend and, unlike many others, wanted nothing but to be accepted in return.

Kristoff had mixed feelings about his family and his life in general. Kristoff did not want to follow in the footsteps of many of the males in his family. He felt as if they were all cold-blooded and manipulative and cared for no one other than themselves.

They continue to find ways to hurt innocent people. Kristoff knows that his decision to leave is going to hurt Jae. He feels as if leaving is the best alternative for him. Kristoff decided to move away to make a fresh start. He no longer wanted to live a life of crime, lies, and secrecy. Jae did not want to lose Kristoff again, but she knew deep down inside it was best for him to leave. She did not want him to end up in jail or dead like many other assassins. Kristoff's decision to leave impacted his parents. Christopher vowed to change his life. Christopher became a member of the church that Jae attended on a regular basis with the Hollermans. He decided to leave the League, and he went back to school. He got a job working 9 to 5 to take care of his family. Jae got her teaching certificate, and Christopher obtained his degree in pharmacy. They wanted their family to have an ordinary life. Jae would soon announce the arrival of her second child. They did not want to have any ties with the League.

Rellik and Collin continued to operate the League. They recruited and trained others to work for the New World Order. Jewel was paid a salary to train the newly recruited assassins. Edge worked as an independent contractor, where he performed hits on a part-time basis.

THE END

Authors Page

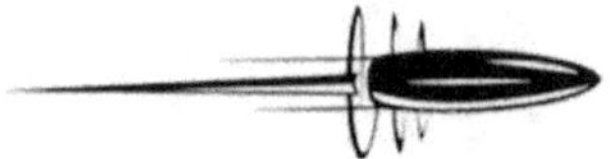

I am honored to be able to introduce myself to you in this capacity. My name is Deiadra Nicole, and I am an author and an aspiring actress. I began narrating fictional short stories at the age of seven years old. It wasn't until high school, upon entering a talent competition, that I began to assess my skills as an author. After graduating from college, I began auditioning for acting gigs. I became interested in writing for television. I would often find myself rewriting my lines to adapt to the way that I felt the storyline should end. I was encouraged to submit my literary works to television to display my writing capabilities. I had many stories to tell, but I had nothing on paper to share tangibly. I found myself writing pages of material with no one to share them or no place to submit them. I was encouraged to publish my literary works. This is the first of many more books to come. I hope that my book(s) will not only meet but exceed your expectations. I am grateful for this platform to be able to showcase my talent. Thank you for your support.